INTERDIMENSIONS

Interdimensions

VOL. 1

2024 GEN CON WRITERS' SYMPOSIUM

LINDA D. ADDISON
JENNIFER BROZEK
RICHARD LEE BYERS
BRANDON CRILLY
RICHARD DANSKY
ANTHONY W. EICHENLAUB
SARAH HANS
GABRIELLE HARBOWY
AKIS LINARDOS

KAREN MENZEL
DANIEL MYERS
RAVEN OAK
CAT RAMBO
JASON SANFORD
LASHAWN M. WANAK
GREGORY A. WILSON
BRYAN YOUNG

EDITED BY TOIYA KRISTEN FINLEY

Atthis Arts
Detroit, Michigan

INTERDIMENSIONS

Copyright © 2024 by Toiya Kristen Finley

All rights reserved. Except as permitted under the US Copyright Act of 1976, no part of this publication may be reproduced, stored in a retrieval system, or transmitted in any form or by any means electronic, mechanical, photocopying, recording, or otherwise, without written permission of the copyright holders.

Cover Illustration by Alex Steffen

Published by Atthis Arts, LLC
Detroit, Michigan
atthisarts.com

ISBN 978-1-961654-23-5

Each story in this collection is copyrighted © 2024 by the story's author.

GEN CON is a registered trademark of Gen Con, LLC.

Content notes are listed in the back of the collection.

Contents

Foreword by Toiya Kristen Finley vii

All Time Is Now *by Linda D. Addison* 1

All Things Fixed *by Anthony W. Eichenlaub* 12

Who We Were in the Mirror *by Karen Menzel* 26

Painted World of Witch and Wizard *by Akis Linardos* 41

Memento Miri *by Daniel Myers* 55

You Need Not Fear *by Brandon Crilly* 69

Turnkey *by Richard Lee Byers* 84

One Kind of Many, Undefined by Them *by Jason Sanford* . . . 93

Eye of the Beholder *by Jennifer Brozek and Raven Oak* 116

The Grandmother Tale *by LaShawn M. Wanak* 129

For a Thousand Silver Blessings *by Bryan Young* 140

Kicking Santa's Ass *by Richard Dansky* 155

The Goblin's Locket *by Gregory A. Wilson* 165

Hands Are for Helping *by Sarah Hans* 181

All the Light in the Room *by Gabrielle Harbowy* 193

Pots of a Color Yet Unknown *by Cat Rambo* 208

Foreword

Toiya Kristen Finley

I attended my first Gen Con and the Writers' Symposium in 2017. I'd been invited as a guest, brought in specifically to talk about video game writing. Since I'd never been to the con, I didn't know what to expect. What amazed me was the range of topics covered (genres and media, a plethora of writing topics, the business life and personal life of being a writer) and the extremely knowledgeable and gifted people I shared panels with. Every year I've attended the Symposium, the guests have shared the wealth of their insights with new writers, seasoned writers, and those looking for their first fiction sales.

I became a member of the Symposium's organizing committee for the 2023 con. I work with dedicated, hardworking people (more hard work than you could ever know) who want to ensure that anyone coming to the Writers' Symposium experiences a spectrum of ideas and skills. That will now include our guests' work on the page, as we are bringing back the Symposium anthology. You've heard their insights. They've given their time and energy sharing their best practices and passions. In this volume, you'll see how they express themselves through their stories.

The Symposium's last anthology was *Carnage & Consequences: Stories from the Gen Con Writer's Symposium Authors*, published in 2011 and edited by Marc Tassin. I'm now the editor of *Interdimensions: Stories from the Gen Con Writers' Symposium*, and I'm honored to present to you stories from our guests, including Linda D. Addison, a 2024 Special Guest.

This anthology could not exist without our publisher, Atthis Arts. I'm grateful to EDE Bell and Christopher Bell for revitalizing it. I'd also like to thank the readers for our submissions: E.D.E. Bell, Alexander Bevier, Marie Bilodeau, Gary Kloster, Karen Menzel, Fred Wan, LaShawn M. Wanak, and Gregory Wilson. *Interdimensions* could not exist without you.

Toiya Kristen Finley
Interdimensions Editor
June 1, 2024

INTERDIMENSIONS

All Time Is Now
(for Nancy Kress)

Linda D. Addison

I am at the Order of the Hand's doorstep—again. Now is pressing against me, creeping closer as each second goes by. I stand with the cloaked waiting to worship their absentee Zachary and carrier of the Hand that signs the true history of the world. I am Zachary, my left hand is the Hand.

The Order's meeting place is an old brick building with a dome roof that looks like the churches I've seen in the vids of the 1990s. After the Crop Nanovirus mutations of 2352 made the cost of real food as high as precious stones, the Order's always had two lines of people. One entrance for the hungry and another for the followers of the Hand.

Tapping a pattern on my left wrist activates the web of implants that still my hand for a short period of time, storing the signals from my brain. Science that can't explain how or why my hand signs random facts as it marches through time gave me this small gift. After three hours, the automatic release kicks in to prevent seizures that come when my hand doesn't complete the circuit.

Even though it's dangerous for me to be here, I can't ever remember really feeling safe. I've spent the last ten years of my life moving from one secure house to another, since Larry stole me from the government research center when I was eight years old. They still search for me, because like the scientists in the underground group that helps hide us, the government researchers are desperate to understand the quantum connection between the microtubules in my brain and my constantly signing hand.

We walk in silence up the curving staircase to the temple's meeting room, each of us wearing dark hooded cloaks. Each called Zachary or Larry. The cloaks are more than ritual; they signify the Order's commitment to providing a way for Larry and I to hide in the open. Members of the Order have the reputation of being fanatical about the privacy of the cloak. They have proven their passion, helped by rich supporters paying for legal aid, in the courtrooms and the blood they've spilled on the street.

I sit on the hardwood floor with the others. Soon the room is full. A carpet of silent, hooded people. There is one piece of furniture in the meeting room, an empty wood stool near the door. A green handprint is on the center of the stool. A child's handprint.

A small, hooded figure enters and sits on the stool. The figure raises its left hand, palm facing us. Everyone's attention is on that small, brown hand.

The child's hand starts to sign in the modified sign language my hand has introduced to the world. The fingers deftly move in the air—stretching, flexing, clenching, the hand dipping at the wrist. The faint sound of hands moving under the rough cloth of the robes whispers in the air as a few sign along with the child.

(... july 24 1214 832 pm   brookesville england jonathan glantz enters blue bane tavern   kotka finland lappa ship sinks 14 drown chad africa mbuji mayi born ...)

This is one of the earlier recorded passages. My heart races. The pacing of the small hand is remarkably even. The hand tirelessly recites dates, times, facts arranged in the usual uneven, forward jumps that my hand signs. Almost half an hour later, the small hand signals the end by repeating the beginning of the passage.

The reciter pushes the hood back from his face. A cloud of tightly curled black hair frames a dark brown face, large clear eyes, round nostrils, full lips—so beautiful, so calm. He's about ten years old, but with eyes so full of peace a chill goes up my back. If only they knew how confused and angry I've been most of my life.

In all the writing created about me and the Hand, Larry wouldn't allow my feelings or opinions. He believed I would be safer, more whole, if the world wasn't analyzing my thoughts along with the words my hand pours out.

The child sings in a gentle voice,

> "We are each Zachary and Larry,
> The blessed Hand brings
> the words of What Was,
> we wait for
> What will Be.
>
> We walk in hooded darkness
> so they can walk in
> daylight."

He stands, replaces his hood and leaves the room. I want to rush after him, look into his peaceful eyes one more time, but I know the rules. I stand and file out of the room with the others.

The large outer hall is filled with children playing, throwing balls, flying little handmade planes in the air. Each child similar in size as the child that spoke to us, each child wearing a cloak.

I sigh. The Order plays out their ritual perfectly. I walk down the stairway with other men and women shrouded in cloaks. I want to throw off my hood and yell, "I'm Zachary, not holy, just a human!" What would they do? Surround me to hide me. Touch me. Not touch me?

In the street I walk quickly past beggars and the wall of street tents leaning against every building, shelter to the homeless. Our car is waiting around the corner.

"skipEE, take me home," I whisper to our private network aide.

"Yes, Zach, 27 minutes to arrival," says a soft female voice in my ear implant.

Fatigue builds as the car passes the endless sidewalk tents under flickering streetlights and takes the ramp to the almost empty highway, then an exit to a country road. I struggle to stay awake watching the shadows of tree tops against a full moon night sky roll by. I take a deep breath when we turn on to the private road, go through two security gates and pull up to the side entrance of the large house.

I know Larry will be angry. I saw it in my waking memories this morning. I enter the living room. Larry is sitting with his back to me, scanning the headlines on a floating VR screen. His wide shoulders, thick neck, and stout body remind me of an athlete—an aging, graying athlete. I can see the tension in his shoulders. I often wonder what his life would have been if he didn't have to shuttle the sad little boy with the moving hand around this planet?

"You were gone a long time," Larry snaps, without turning.

"But you always know exactly where I am because of skipEE."

I throw the cloak to the couch and sit opposite him.

Larry closes the screen and punches the desk.

I don't react. This morning, after the mini-seizure, I saw this day unfold, his anger, us being taken from this place and then . . .

"Why do you take these chances? I do everything to keep you safe and even let you go out without me, but to go to a building filled with followers—"

"I know, but I had to go to this meeting," I say as calmly as possible.

"Why?" Larry asks, his voice louder.

I stare unblinking, suddenly unable to focus.

"The muscle lock, Zach." Larry's voice softens.

"skipEE, release hand lock." I rest my left arm in my lap. My left hand and fingers dance in the air, while the implant transmits saved messages to skipEE's secure network.

(. . . november 26 2595 213 pm   paris france interest rates triple   topeka kansas jim thompson accepted at michigan state university of bio planetology . . .)

"Why did you have to go to the meeting?" Larry asks again.

I looked down at my hand, tirelessly moving as it has every moment of my life. It has jumped three years.

(... june 5 2598 730 am   district of new found town india 1593 girl babies born carbiotics factory   hoboken new jersey 14226 containers produced a second ...)

The Hand. Not my hand. I've always wondered if my parents knew or they left me at the orphanage because they couldn't take care of me, like so many other parents in our suffering world.

"I had memories of this day when I woke up this morning," I say.

"You mean a dream?" Larry asks.

"No, I saw this day like a movie I was remembering from the moment I got out of the bed. And I've been having mini-seizures for two weeks."

Larry sits next to me on the couch. He doesn't look surprised.

"The doctors told you to expect these seizures as we get closer to Now, didn't they?" I ask.

Larry runs his hand through his thinning hair. "They've said many things over the years, guesses about you and this hand. Too many guesses to worry you with, but they never mentioned you being able to see things before they happen."

Suddenly my jaw clenches close as intense burning races up and down my spine, bringing tears to my eyes, then just as suddenly, the mini-seizure ends. I see more details of how this day will unfold.

"Should I contact the doctors?" Larry asks.

"Not yet," I say. "But I could use some water."

"I'll be right back," he says, and quickly leaves the room.

Another shudder grabs me. I dig into the arm of the chair with my right hand while intense tingling runs through my body. My left hand is unaffected.

I knew that one was coming. I didn't want Larry here when it started so close to the last one.

It ends quickly, and for the first time in my life, I know what my hand is signing without looking at it. I can feel a flow of words and numbers through me like leaves on a stream. All of my life, I've been just another observer until this moment.

Larry returns with a glass of water.

I drink it slowly as he sits next to me.

"Larry, something is changing inside of me." I tell him as much about the knowing that I can put into words; how these seizures bring me more knowledge each time.

"Have you seen what will happen when the hand reaches Now?" he asks.

"No." I hesitate. "Another seizure is coming. A big one. Don't be afraid." I slide to the floor.

"What can I do?" He sits bunched up in the chair, all tense muscles and clenched fists.

"Just be here," I say.

He sits beside me on the floor and clasps my right hand tightly.

"Don't worry, I'll be alright," I say.

I feel the thick carpet against my back as a wave of energy rises from my stomach.

i am floating   words float around me like infinite stars in the night sky   the words my hand has already signed dance like white light among infinity   i am in the center   i am not alone   every one that lives, has lived, and will live is with me   i cannot see them   i feel them   we share all history   all memories   their lives   my life   all part of a river that flows through me   i am at a point of existence   in all of existence   feelings   some mine some not   flow in the river   happy sad hungry full confusion knowing not knowing love hate loneliness pain pain pain joy joy joy the end of loneliness   completeness...

I feel a softness against my back, like floating on thick gel. I open my eyes. I am on a scan platform in a brightly lit room. Larry stands next to me. There are others in the room in light grey jumpsuits.

"Zach, are you all right?" Larry asks.

I nod slowly. "How long?" I say hoarsely, my throat painfully dry.

"Three—" Larry looks at his watch, "no—four hours. I had to call our doctors. Your pulse would race and then slow down. Too slow. I was afraid you were dying." He helped me sip water.

"Hours." I shake my head. "It felt like seconds."

"They airlifted us to this secure facility," he said. "I know you said no doctors, but—"

"It's okay. I knew we would end this day here."

One of the doctors I don't recognize comes over. "You saw this before it occurred?"

"Yes."

"Why is this happening?" Larry asks.

"We're not sure." The doctor snaps her fingers and draws a square in the air. Images of a brain glow in the middle of the VR panel. "The pathways from his right hemisphere are showing undefinable frequency signatures that weren't there before. You both know we've been studying for years vibrations from his microtubules that imply quantum activity in Zach's brain, but we don't know how to put it all together and explain his hand signing facts that he can't possibly know."

They turn to my hand.

(. . . september 28 2598 330 pm   magdeburg germany kimberly torgau conceives third child   penha guanabara tora footwear factory produces 446 size 8 red shoes . . .)

"We are less than an hour from the hand catching up with our present time," she says. "There's no way to know what that jump in time will be."

"Isn't there anything you can do?" Larry says, raising his voice.

The doctor shakes her head. "Anything we've considered could cause harm to Zach. You did the best thing calling us. This is the safest place for him." She walks away to join others that are looking at my stats on their monitors.

I turn to Larry. Of all the images I remember from the last seizure, I have the memory of his deep feelings of guilt for telling his supervisors about the signing infant at the state orphanage. He convinced them to let him take care of me when they took me to the research center. I also felt his decision to get me out of their hands when he saw the experiments they ran to figure out what was happening to me. Larry never told me about his part in my being taken from the orphanage.

I try to sit up, but I'm too weak. A mixture of fear and surrender twists my stomach into knots.

"Larry," I whisper.

He steps in close.

"I love you so much for giving your life to me all these years. Please find a way to live without guilt, a way to enjoy your life. I know what you did when I was a baby."

Larry's eyes widen in shock and sadness. "I'm sorry."

"I'm not. I can't imagine anyone else who could have taken such good care of me. I see now it's what had to happen."

"I don't understand," Larry says, his voice cracking.

Now is one minute away.

I want to try to explain, but I can't because a seizure starts.

I am the Witness.
My Hand the key.
The River of All Time flows
   in me to The Hand.
   in all humans.
Everything I am:
   my feelings, sensations, memories
   join the river of all human memories.
The Hand has shown many humans
   something outside the known exists,
   something other than the slow death

we have created on this planet and in each other.
I am complete for the first time.
My hand stops moving for the first time.
I can't see Larry or the room—
   everything   is   turning   to   light ...

Linda D. Addison grew up in Philadelphia and began weaving stories at an early age. Ms Addison is the first African-American recipient of the world renowned HWA Bram Stoker Award and has received five awards for collections: *The Place of Broken Things* written with Alessandro Manzetti; *Four Elements* written with Charlee Jacob, Marge Simon, and Rain Graves; *How To Recognize A Demon Has Become Your Friend* short stories and poetry; *Being Full of Light, Insubstantial*; *Consumed, Reduced to Beautiful Grey Ashes*. In 2018, she received the HWA Lifetime Achievement Award. In 2020, Addison was designated SFPA Grand Master of Fantastic Poetry. She coedited *Sycorax's Daughters* anthology of horror fiction & poetry by African-American women with Kinitra Brooks PhD and Susana Morris PhD, which was a HWA Bram Stoker finalist in the Anthology category. She currently lives in Arizona and has published over 400 poems, stories and articles. Look for her story in the *Black Panther: Tales of Wakanda* anthology (Titan/Marvel). Her site: www.LindaAddisonWriter.com.

All Things Fixed

Anthony W. Eichenlaub

Nothing was ever broken in the city-station of Nicodemia.

The city's AI, Trinity, kept everything functioning. Lights and doors were repaired promptly. Holes patched. The buildings lining the great central spiral stayed perfect as the pulse of life pumped through fibersteel veins. Everything functioned as it should. Always.

Everything was always broken in the city-station of Nicodemia.

That's where I came in. "Jude Demarco," I said. "All things found, all things fixed."

"Lance Magnusson." The short man peered at me like he might bolt if I twitched funny. His hands were calloused and beard unkempt. "Is it true you're excommunicated?"

"If you're looking for Trinity-certified repairs—"

"No," he interrupted. "I mean, we've tried that. We need someone outside the system."

I was excommunicated, but not by the Catholic Church. Years ago, I chose to sacrifice a transport ship rather than risk the whole city, and the church-designed AI, Trinity, shunned me for it. It was a bad decision surrounded by worse ones, and just because I couldn't win didn't mean I didn't lose. Trinity's Karma system distributed food, housing, and clothing based on the perceived deeds of a heavily surveilled population. Its mandate was to support body, soul, and community of every citizen of the space station, but it ignored me completely. It didn't turn on lights or open doors for me. To Trinity, I was nothing. Excommunicated.

"What's broke?" I asked.

"Everything."

Magnusson led me down the long central road of Heavy Nicodemia's spiral, alongside the rumbling trolleys and the worn-down crowds of dock workers and tradesmen. Down at the bottom of Nicodemia's lowest segment, the station's spin gravity was heaviest, homes were least desirable, and moods were most dour. The night was young, but the false sky was filled with a starlight glow. Clinging mist filled the air, resulting from the cool night air striking the humidity rising from the fish farms below.

When we were near the Docks, Magnusson veered into the maze of streets lined with stubby tenements.

"You live in the Yards?" I asked.

"Right on the edge," Magnusson explained.

"It's dark," I said. The tenement in front of us was a silhouette against the gray gloom of night. It should have been crawling with activity this early in the evening.

Trinity's algorithms favored community even here among the poorest districts of Heavy Nicodemia. *Especially* here.

"You said you had this fixed before?" I said.

"Twice."

"Show me."

The conduit junction was a fibersteel box at the foot of the tenement complex. Its lock was cracked wide open, and the wires inside had been expertly spliced.

I became aware of eyes watching me from the hazy windows of the tenement. Men, women, and children all peered at me from behind drab curtains. They needed this fix. They were desperate.

"Who did it?" I asked.

"It was the Ghost of the Yards." A woman stepped around the corner. She was built sturdy as an industrial winch, and her brown hair was tied in a ponytail.

"There's no proof of that," said Magnusson.

The woman was undeterred. "Folks saw a skinny man, all bones and elbows. White as a carp's belly. That's the Ghost."

At my raised eyebrow, Magnusson explained, "This is Parva Gardner. She's our self-appointed security."

"Appointed by vote," said Gardner.

The tension between the two hung in the air, so I poked at it. "This Ghost have a name?"

"Doesn't need one," Gardner said.

"Why not take this up with him?" I asked.

Magnusson glanced at the eyes peering out at us. "We're not here because we're brave."

"Why *are* you here?" They lived in one of the worst tenement buildings in the city.

The two glanced at each other, but it was Gardner who said, "Trinity put us here." Their Karma was trash.

I said, "All it would take is one good deed, and you could move away."

"What if we were wrong?" Magnusson asked.

If their Karma dropped any further, they might need to move somewhere worse—if there was somewhere worse. That explained their cowardice. They'd probably all been bitten by Trinity's inconsistent judgments.

It also explained why they wouldn't fix their own junction. Trinity would dock the Karma of anyone doing so without proper work orders. That's why they needed someone excommunicated. I could fix the junction without waiting for the proper permits.

It was an easy job. After switching the breaker off, I performed the rewiring without much trouble. Magnusson shone a light for me as I worked, but he was careful not to touch anything.

When I finished, I switched the breaker back on, and the tenement building lit up with light and cheers. But Gardner stood with her arms crossed and her brow creased. Magnusson slapped me on the back. He tried to pay me, but I wouldn't take his dimes. The job wasn't done.

I found a nearby shadow, lit a cigarette, leaned against the wall, and waited.

My third cigarette heralded the approach of the Ghost. I recognized the old man by his white pasty skin and wispy hair. He wore a grungy white T-shirt and baggy gray pants—the kind of clothing a person gets when they've bottomed out their Karma. A cheap-looking red gun poked out of his waistband. I wondered what this man had done to earn such poverty.

Body, soul, community. He must have violated one to have such lousy Karma.

The Ghost approached the junction box. Any of the residents of the tenement could have seen him out their window, but they chose ignorance. Seeing him meant confrontation. Confrontation meant risk.

I didn't mind risk.

Smoke lingered in a halo around my head. "Careful to disengage the breaker first."

The Ghost jumped, and the gun was in his hand.

"Easy," I said, showing my empty palms. I stepped from the shadow into the dim cone of light surrounding him. "Nobody's interested in getting shot around here."

The cheap gun didn't waver. It might be a lousy printed weapon, but odds were it could kill well enough. That or it would explode and make a huge mess.

"Lot of folks need this power," I said.

"What's it to you?" the Ghost said.

I moved closer. "Takes a low man to wish for a place this lousy."

His eyes narrowed. "I'm not coveting this place."

"That would be a sin, wouldn't it?" Another step. The gun in his outstretched hand pressed against my chest. "Bad for the Karma."

"Why don't you scram?"

I took his wrist and twisted until he dropped the gun. He let out a piteous yelp. I kicked the gun into the shadows.

He looked up at me through tears. "It was only for a little while. Only a few days!"

"Why?"

He crumpled. His ribcage showed through the holes in his threadbare shirt.

I grabbed his shoulders and made him face me. "I'm going to get to the bottom of this whether you like it or not. Where are you routing this signal to?"

His blubbering answer was a tumble of sobs and phlegm.

I took his jaw in my meaty hand and looked straight into his eyes.

"The Underdocks," he said. "Beneath the salmon farms."

I dropped him and strode into the dark. He followed. The streetlights that ignored me flickered to life ahead of him, dim and dusty in the Nicodemia night. We descended into the Docks.

Funny thing about fish was that they weren't affected by the heavier gravity of the lower sections of the city. They grew just as fat as they would if they were nestled into the loftiest and lightest of the Hallows high above. I followed my nose to the salmon fisheries and found the entrance to the nearby Underdocks.

I asked the Ghost, "How did you know how to reroute that junction?"

He licked his dry lips. "I wasn't always who I am now."

"None of us are."

"Please," he said, "we just want to be left in peace."

"Show me."

The Ghost looked at me with red-rimmed eyes. It was almost enough to break a man's stony heart. It was the kind of kicked-puppy expression that works so well on the religious types up at the church or on bleeding hearts down by the Docks. It was a beggar's look, designed to manipulate.

I wasn't buying it.

The Underdocks sat below shallow fish farms, dripping with damp and smelling of rot. I had to duck as I shouldered my way through the grimy space, but I kept up with the Ghost as he wended his way through narrow tunnels. After several stifling minutes under the weight of tons of water, we emerged into a small utility room.

The Ghost gasped and rushed into the poorly lit space.

She was even paler than the Ghost. Her white hair hung in stringy clumps on the stained pillow, and her lips were pulled back in a grimace. Skinny arms emerged from a thin, tangled blanket, and her hands grasped for the Ghost's, holding them tight when, finally, she found him. The room smelled of human excrement and sweat. A battered wheelchair sat in one corner.

A dark lamp sat next to the woman alongside the discarded remains of several meals. One wall featured a blank screen. Empty medicine bottles were scattered across the floor.

The woman saw me and descended into a fit of coughing.

I knelt by her side and felt her weak pulse writhing under clammy skin. When she stopped coughing, she met my gaze. She didn't speak, but she didn't need to. I could read the pain in her expression as I proceeded through an exam.

"You don't look like a man with medical training," said the Ghost.

"I wasn't always who I am now," I muttered. As a wealthy little snot growing up in the Hallows, I'd foolishly dreamt of the medical profession. If I could fix the sick, I figured I could fix anything.

But this woman was beyond fixing.

"There's a medical bay up at the tenement," I said.

"It won't help," said the Ghost.

"She can be made more comfortable." I gripped the woman's hand, willing my heat to flow into her cold hands.

The Ghost gestured at the screen and the lights. "I *was* making her comfortable."

I stared at the man. His bony jaw was set. His fists were balled at his sides, and while I didn't fear him, I *did* fear what might happen if he tried to start a fight.

"Why is your Karma so low?" I asked.

His fists tightened, but the woman put a gentle hand on his and he calmed. When he finally spoke, it was through gritted teeth. "We used to live up in that tenement. Lorie and I were good citizens. Nothing fancy. We worked the fisheries. I wired junctions, and she tended trout." He glanced at Lorie, and an expression of gentle love flashed across his rugged features. "We were happy for a long time."

Lorie worked her mouth as if she were trying to speak, but the Ghost quieted her.

I said, "What happened?"

"We used to watch vids," the Ghost said. "*Yeoman Chronicles*. Remember that one?" I didn't. A twinkle in Lorie's eyes said she did. "It was our favorite. It was about a place where water covered the whole world, and sailors went on adventures. They sailed and sailed and sailed and never ran into a wall."

Lorie made a choking sound that might have been laughter.

"Then it all fell apart," I prompted.

"Greed," said the Ghost.

Lorie shook her head.

"It was," he insisted. "Started out that we couldn't get the food we liked. Vids were downgraded. Grainy video, crappy sound. My Lorie—" The Ghost took Lorie's hands in his own. "—she deserved better, so I stole a meal from one of the other residents. It was a bad move, and that's when our Karma tanked out totally. We couldn't get into our apartment."

I said, "Good deeds should have rebuilt your Karma."

"Nothing took."

"Body, soul, community," I said. "Come on, there had to be something. Help an old lady across the street or tutor kids at the school."

The Ghost tightened up again. "Nothing worked. I'm telling you, *nothing* worked." Lorie squeezed his hand and said something with her eyes. "That was when they first got security at the tenement. After that, we couldn't even visit."

The pieces clicked into place. "Does that wheelchair work?"

"It does."

"Bring Lorie," I said. "We're getting your home back."

Gardner blocked the entrance to the tenement, scowling. "I got enough trouble without those types coming around."

"They won't be trouble," I promised.

"Ha!" She tilted her head back at the building where the windows shone with the eyes of wary residents. "We know what happens to thieves like them."

"Karma," I said.

"Damn straight."

The Ghost stepped back, pulling Lorie with him, but I gestured for him to stop with an open palm. "Tell me something," I said, "What's the Karma impact for helping someone in need?"

Her eyes narrowed. "It depends on what they deserve."

"Does it? Or does it only matter that they're in need?"

"Everybody knows about the Ghost," said Gardner.

"He's a legend," I said.

"A thief."

I dredged up something from the Bible-taught recesses of my brain. "'Whoever is kind to the poor lends to the Lord and will be paid in full.'"

"'The Lord sends poverty and wealth. He humbles and he exalts,'" Gardner quoted.

"No Lord made these people poor," I said.

"They did it to themselves." Gardner glanced at the building behind her. Curious faces watched from hazy windows. "People need to suffer the effects of their Karma."

I was tiring of this. "One last chance, Gardner. Lorie is dying. She needs a place to stay."

"Get out of here before I make you regret it," Gardner said.

"We're coming in." I waved the Ghost forward. "You don't have any right to stop us."

Gardner drew the Ghost's cheap-looking gun. "Back off."

I raised my hands. "It doesn't need to go down like this."

"People like you always cause trouble for people like us."

"People like *me*? This problem is your making, Gardner. Your Ghost stole from you, so you kicked him out of the tenement. You spread the rumors of the danger he posed so that they'd vote you the security lead. After securing your place in the community, Trinity started to see you as valuable. Am I right so far?"

Magnusson appeared in the doorway. "We don't want this trouble, Gardner."

"Once you were valuable to Trinity," I continued, "you found it beneficial to keep the rumors going. Demonize him. You made him into a legend. You built a community of fear, as if the terrifying, impoverished people might revolt. Your Karma improved because you were the center of that community."

The gun shook in Gardner's hand. More windows opened behind her.

"We won't be leaving," I said. "You made these people afraid of their own poverty. Terrified to bring their own forms of kindness into the world. What if Trinity judged them poorly? Would they end with the same fate as the Ghost?"

"The Ghost threatens us," Gardner said.

"Fear is the only threat. If you embrace him as one of your own—"

"He's a monster!"

"He has a name."

Gardner stared at me, the whites of her eyes glowing in the false moonlight.

"The Ghost is a story you told to rally them around your hate, but he's a real person. Lorie is a real person. They need your help. They need *anyone's* help. Don't you think it's worth helping them up, even if it doesn't improve your own Karma? Even if it's a sacrifice?"

"It's my job to protect my people." She pointed the gun at me, then at the Ghost, then back at me. Her face was flushed, and she trembled with fury.

All of the windows were open now. Magnusson said, "His name is Mr. Guest."

"Lawrence," called an elderly woman in one of the higher windows. "Lawrence Guest."

"That's right," called a man from the bottom floor. "He was one of us."

"He made a mistake," said Magnusson. "I was young when it happened, but I remember people talking about it."

Lawrence Guest, the Ghost, said, "I'm sorry." Tears streamed down his cheeks. "I'm so sorry, Gardner. Can't you forgive me? For Lorie's sake?"

The flush in her face went pale, and the gun lowered by a fraction of an inch.

But Gardner didn't have forgiveness in her heart.

She aimed the gun at Guest. I dove to try to stop her.

Too late.

The gun fired with a snap. A scream. Blood.

Gardner's blood. The shattered remnants of the gun and several fingers fell to the cold ground. I reached her and held her wrists. Her screams turned to cries.

Cries turned to words. "It's justice," she said again and again. "It's justice."

༄

Lorie died a week later in the warm comfort of Guest's arms. They watched episodes of *Yeoman Chronicles*, which turned out to be an old satire poking fun at the adventures of early spacefarers.

"He has a room now," said Magnusson. "Trinity accepts him as a resident."

"The legend is broken," I said. "The only thing keeping him down was that a community was built around vilifying him."

"That's horrible."

I shrugged. "It's what we make it."

"What about Gardner?" Magnusson said.

"She lost two fingers. Maybe that's penance enough for her sins. Maybe it isn't."

Magnusson glanced at Guest's room. "Will she go after him again?"

I thought about that for a while. "It was never really about him."

"But will he be safe? Is this fixed?"

"Fixed? Maybe. It's as fixed as it's going to be." With that, I made my way out of the tenement and through the Yards into the central spiral. I'd fixed one broken twist of Trinity's logic, but the truth was that everything was always broken in the city-station of Nicodemia. Nobody was ever really safe.

But nothing was ever broken in the city-state of Nicodemia. Everything worked exactly as designed.

Anthony W. Eichenlaub's stories have appeared in *Daily Science Fiction*, *On-Spec Magazine*, *Little Blue Marble*, and numerous anthologies including *A Punk Rock Future* and *The Community of Magic Pens*. His novels range from Minnesota technothrillers to the sci-fi noir tales of Jude Demarco in a city-station where sinners are saints and good deeds are a commodity. His philosophy is that even the most serious science fiction should be absurdly fun. Anthony teaches writing in his local community and is a teaching artist at the Loft Literary Center in Minneapolis. In his spare time, Anthony enjoys landscaping, woodworking, and long walks with his lazy dog. More about his work can be found at anthonyeichenlaub.com.

Who We Were in the Mirror
Karen Menzel

Eleanor hadn't seen Margie for ten years, but her sister's sour expression hadn't changed. Her twin had the same brown-going-grey hair and crow's feet gathering at the edges of her eyes as Eleanor did, but where Eleanor was used to seeing her own smiling mouth, Margie's lips were pressed tightly. Eleanor's high school bestie had said Margie was the poster child for "resting bitch face," except that was giving her sister too much credit. "Resting" implied that bitch face went away sometimes.

"Hi, Margie," Eleanor said, forcing as much warmth into her tone as she was able. Her sister's style had grown up from standard garage band Gen Xer to what the kids these days called "killer." She had a French bob with very short bangs, a micro fringe, Eleanor thought it was called, and black barbell plugs in her earlobes. Black hornrims and a black manicure made her cropped T and distressed jeans look upscale. She looked good. Eleanor had to admit, she looked better than Eleanor did in her drama-teacher business casual.

"Call me Mags." Margie's words were clipped as she swung her suitcase into Eleanor's open trunk.

The train whistle blew as her sister climbed into the passenger seat. By chance, Eleanor slammed the trunk shut at the same time Margie shut the car door. Just like that, Eleanor was back in a childhood of matching dresses, finishing each other's sentences, and complicated feelings.

"Promise me you'll take care of Margie. She needs your good influence." Her mother's dying words echoed. The train pulled out of the station, racing on to somewhere else, leaving Eleanor alone with her sister and her unfulfilled promise. Eleanor climbed into the car with her silent sister, buckled her seatbelt, and rolled up her window. She was who she was, and her sister was who she was, and that was that.

ᛋ

"How much more do we have to do?" Margie smeared dirt across her forehead with a sweaty hand and pulled aside her face mask to take a few breaths of clean air outside their mother's basement. She looked like an extra from *Fury Road*.

Eleanor put down the box full of moth-eaten, funky-smelling stuffed animals. She choked back what she really wanted to say, which was that she'd already spent a month of weekends hauling worthless junk out of their parents' decaying farmhouse. That was on top of weeks of dealing with their mother's end-of-life details, arranging the funeral Margie didn't bother to come to. Years of being on call during their mother's decline.

"I promised Mom you'd get final say on all our old stuff, then a look at everything else before the auction company comes." Her mother's will stated they were to split all assets, but they had to sort through their childhood toys together. "We're almost done. There's only a couple more boxes."

Margie frowned, but to her credit, she put her mask back on and went into the musty basement for another load. Though they were twins, Margie had clearly spent more time at the gym than Eleanor. Margie seemed to have endless stamina, even though Eleanor was lighter on her feet from teaching dance and drama.

By late afternoon, their childhood was strewn across the backyard like colorful guts. The dumpster Eleanor had rented was half full of moldy Cabbage Patch dolls, busted Fisher Price toys, and enough Pound Puppies to reenact *101 Dalmatians*. None of it was in good enough shape for eBay, even if either of them wanted the hassle.

Margie came out of the basement with a large open box. A carved wooden case stuck out of the top.

"Oh, man." Eleanor remembered it well. "Mirror Labyrinth. Is this the one from that creepy flea market, where I thought the guy was going to sell us a monkey's paw?"

"Yeah." Margie grunted. She chewed on her upper lip, revealing her lower incisors. An unsightly habit, their mother had said.

Margie set the box on the wobbly picnic table and Eleanor joined her, trying not to notice they both sat at the same time and heaved identical sighs. Mirror, indeed.

Eleanor fished the game case out of the box, which was piled high with what looked like Margie's old diaries. The maze-inscribed game, despite being dusty, was in perfect condition, the backward "R" in the title just how Eleanor remembered it. She traced the lines of the maze with one finger while Margie fiddled with the latch.

"Man, remember how long it took us ..." Eleanor started, pressing down the two knobs on the back.

"... just to figure out how to open it?" Margie finished, pressing the latch mechanism. The box clicked, and Margie opened the case, revealing a jangle of pieces inside. The hinges creaked like a door opening to a cellar, but the inside of the game smelled like metal and plastic, not mold and decay.

"My guy!" Eleanor plucked the sorceress in the red dress from a tangle of dungeon walls. The original owner of the game had painstakingly painted each piece, not the blobby enamel their father had used on his models, but with oil paint that smelled faintly of shoe polish. Every piece had been shaded with attention to realism, even showing how the flame on the end of the sorceress's staff lit up her face. Without thinking about it, Eleanor twirled in place and cast an imaginary spell with an invisible wand, realizing, even as she did so, she'd performed the action hundreds of times in front of the high school choir. Huh. How had she forgotten Terabithia the Sorceress had inspired the motion?

"Mine too," Margie whispered. The massive orc with huge muscles rested reverently between her black fingernails. It was supposed to be one of the Labyrinth's bad guys, but it had been Margie's favorite, so they'd decided to change the rules, switching it for the armored knight. The ambitious sculptor had created the orc with an improbably large axe that meant the mini fell over all the time. Margie had always held it between two fingers, just like she was doing now. Eleanor had to admit, it looked like it belonged there.

"We should play. For old time's sake," Eleanor said, suddenly wanting to more than she had wanted anything in a long time.

Eleanor hadn't realized her sister was smiling until Margie's smile faded. Margie put down the orc, took the sorceress from Eleanor, and stuffed them back into the box, closing the lid.

"No. We have work to do." And just like that, Margie put her mask on and went back into the basement, leaving Eleanor alone, surrounded by garbage. Exactly like the last ten years. Just when Eleanor had started to hope they might be able to recapture something elusive that she couldn't name, Margie walked way.

Margie had *loved* Mirror Labyrinth. Eleanor remembered her asking to play it just about every day until they both left for college. Why would she refuse to play it now? Eleanor traced the maze again with her fingertips. It had been the only toy they'd had that was clearly marketed for boys.

"No girls of mine will play violent games!" her mother had said after they'd come home with it. In a rare act of defiance, they'd snatched it from the curb before the garbage truck came and hidden it in the basement. Hours and hours they'd played, their mother none-the-wiser. The game had come with quest cards and different layouts for the labyrinth, colorful dice and monsters to defeat. They'd barely ever used the actual rules—just imagined together. The elf sorceress and the orc warrior, back to back, impossible to defeat, facing down the world together. When had that changed? It hadn't been sudden—a slow drift of screaming matches between Margie and Mom, different hobbies, different friend groups. Well, Eleanor had hobbies and a friend group. Margie had her diaries. Eleanor was in drama club, carried on with their childhood dance lessons, and ran with a big group of girlfriends. Margie, well . . . She spent all her teen years with her nose in either a novel or writing in a journal. She probably would have fallen in with a bad crowd, except there weren't any in their town. All *good* kids, as her mother always said. Eleanor had joked with her bestie that Margie never replied to her because she was too busy finishing her memoir, and didn't bother to come to Mom's funeral because she was in the middle of writing an important scene about how hateful her family was.

The truth was, Eleanor had no idea why Margie had missed the funeral, nor what had happened between her and their mother, nor why Margie had ignored her all these years. It was incomprehensibly selfish. She wasn't even sure why Margie was here now because it wasn't like there was that much to inherit. Her style spoke of a trendy life, maybe not a rich one, but she seemed well. Margie or, actually, *Mags*, seemed like she was doing just fine. Eleanor wished, for just a moment, she could cast a massive fireball and burn up the artifacts of long-gone happiness. Magic missile her grief and fatigue away. Teleport far away from here.

But no.

Margie plopped another box of their shared childhood on the ground beside her. So, like always, Eleanor had responsibilities. She reluctantly left Mirror Labyrinth to help her estranged sister.

"Gorgon! Now!" Terabithia the Sorceress screamed. The huge orc, her best friend, screamed his battle cry and the double-sided battleaxe clove the minotaur's head in two. The hair of Gorgon's battle-crest rose in the air, sparking with static electricity as Terabithia readied a spell to take down the minotaur's minions. Gorgon pivoted to the side, giving her a clear shot down the long hallway as she let loose her lightning bolt. A dozen kobolds fell dying or dead, and the smell of roast meat made her wrinkle her nose. Gorgon laughed, his deep voice echoing through the labyrinth, and pulled a sizzling leg off one of the fallen foes.

"Lunch!" he said, opening his tusked mouth.

"Don't you dare!" Terabithia said. "We don't have time to stop and eat. We have to defeat the green dragon before Mom gets back from choir practice."

But Gorgon only laughed and ate his fill.

Eleanor woke from the dream smelling burned meat and, for a moment, didn't know where she was. The familiar shapes of her mother's bedroom gradually resolved in the early morning light. That's right. She'd chosen to sleep in Mom's room because Margie wouldn't even go into it; therefore, Margie slept in the only other room in the house—the twins' old bedroom. Though Eleanor half-believed Margie would have gladly slept in the car instead. The bright pink and yellow bedroom with Care Bear sheets was like a sealed time capsule.

"Margie?" Eleanor called as she wandered into the kitchen. Bacon was sizzling in a glass casserole. Her sister was the only person she knew who cooked bacon in the oven. Margie slammed shut her laptop as Eleanor entered. She even made sleep-tussled look trendy. Maybe the hair cut was impervious to bedhead. She noticed a tattoo she hadn't seen yesterday peeking out of a rip in the jeans. A polyhedron with numbers on each triangle.

"Okay. It's not like I'm going to snoop or something." She belatedly remembered Margie's preferred name. "Mags."

"I . . ." Margie stopped talking, but Eleanor had no idea how to finish her sentence for her. She slid bread into the toaster instead, then sat at the table where her sister looked at the sizzling bacon.

"I'm sorry," Eleanor said, though she wasn't sure what she was apologizing for, exactly.

"Yeah," Margie said. They both reached for an avocado at the same time and stopped.

"I can't . . ." Margie stopped again.

Eleanor waited. It wasn't always a strategy that worked with Margie when they'd been kids—more often than not, Margie would simply wander off and start reading a book. Eleanor waited, made two avocado toasts with bacon, and slid one plate in front of her sister.

"I'm not *like* you," Margie ground out.

Eleanor scoffed. "Actually, being like each other is the literal definition of identical twins." But, when Margie didn't answer, Eleanor felt guilty. "I'm sorry," she said again. "Please. Tell me?"

Margie sighed heavily and took a big bite. "I'm not avocado toasts and pumpkin lattes."

Eleanor's eyes slid to the Keurig, which indeed smelled like pumpkin spice. "Too cool?"

"No. I'm too uncool."

Eleanor waited, knowing that her younger self would never have had the patience.

"Do you remember playing that game when we were kids?" Margie asked.

"Uno? Connect Four?" Eleanor said, even though she knew that wasn't want Margie meant.

"Jerk." The corner of Margie's mouth turned up. "Mirror Labyrinth."

"Of course, I remember."

"Well, I mean, do you remember Gorgon?"

"Your guy? Yeah, sure I do." Eleanor smiled.

"Playing Gorgon was the only time I felt like . . . me."

"What do you mean?" Eleanor stared at her twin, no idea at all what she might say next. She remembered how much fun they both had. When they were playing Mirror Labyrinth, Margie was impulsive and funny. In fact, now that she thought about it, playing that game was some of the best times they'd had together. "If you liked pretending so much, why didn't you join drama club like me?"

"Yeah, how often did you get to play an orc in drama club?"

Eleanor thought about it. "Well, never." Theirs was a small-town school, so they didn't get to do as many productions as bigger towns. Also, the theater teacher was really into tragedies. The closest Eleanor had gotten to something like Mirror Labyrinth was playing a fairy in *Midsummer Night's Dream*. "It wasn't the coolest club, but it was good clean fun, and appropriate. Good for young ladies."

Margie shook her head. "Grab your toast." She tucked her laptop under her arm, walked out of the kitchen.

༄

Her sister led her to the dumpster, where Eleanor recognized the box of diaries crammed into the corner.

"Pick one," Margie said.

Eleanor finished her toast and opened one of the colorfully decorated covers. Gorgon rode hard for the castle, a screaming pack of banshees on his heels. She flipped a few pages. Gorgon saved Terabithia from an evil soul-stealing wizard. Page after page of her sister's cramped words, the little-kid writing so like Eleanor's had been.

"Margie! This is awesome! You can't throw these away. You were so creative." Eleanor seized another journal. The handwriting was more sophisticated, the dates from their high school years. Gorgon was in prison, an evil queen his jailor. Terabithia was her mind slave. Uncomfortable, Eleanor kept reading. Terabithia left Gorgon in the dungeon, distracted by a glittering group of chatting fairies named Jennifer or Amy or Michelle. "Oh."

"Remember how I wanted fencing lessons, and Mom wouldn't let me? Martial arts? No."

Eleanor nodded. She also now remembered how often she herself had said no when Margie asked to play Mirror Labyrinth together. How her sister became more and more quiet, and they spent less time together. How other girls in their class would talk about Margie being weird.

"I'm a lot more like Gorgon than I was ever like you or Mom." Margie opened the laptop.

The document on the screen was pages of dialogue, but it also looked kind of like a multiple-choice test. She kept scrolling.

"Is this . . . a script? Screenplay?"

"This is for a video game. I've also written for roleplaying games. I cosplay. I do some voice acting. And, well, I'm a professional game master too."

"Cos what? Master who?"

Margie told her about a world of conventions, something called actual play podcasts, and how she'd married a woman who owned a game store where people paid her to guide them through games.

"So you're a professional game player?" Eleanor asked.

Margie smirked. "You could say that."

Eleanor didn't know what to say. "Why didn't you tell me?" *Why weren't you here?*

"Come with me."

Eleanor followed her sister into their old bedroom. The walls were bright sunshine yellow, the bunk bed bright pink. Honestly, it still looked really cute with the Sunshine Bear and Cheer Bear bedspreads. Margie slid open the closet doors, which spilled white and pink tutus from their years of dance lessons.

"Tell me there is room in this bedroom for Gorgon the orc."

She had a point. Now that she thought about it, she did

remember their mother cracking down on Margie's "flights of fancy" as she called them. *Why can't you be more like your sister?* She remembered Margie asking to watch fantasy movies and science fiction TV shows, but Mother saying those were too violent. The Disney Channel was good enough for her daughters. Good clean fun, and appropriate. Good for young ladies. Eleanor groaned and rubbed her temples. She was beginning to see Margie's point.

"Does your wife, um, play games too?" As she asked, she realized the question was stupid. The woman owned a game store, after all.

Margie blushed, then laughed at the look on Eleanor's face, and Eleanor had the feeling her sister knew exactly what she'd just been thinking.

"Why didn't you tell me?" Eleanor didn't know if she meant Margie's wife or about how important their imagination games had been to Margie.

"Tell me, do you know anyone gay in this town?"

Eleanor had to admit she knew people she thought were probably gay, but gay in the no-one-talked-about-it-yet-everyone-accepted-they-were-gay kind of way. Gay by omission wasn't progressive. There wasn't anything like a gay culture. That she knew of, anyway. Certainly no one she was friends with. Eleanor's face flushed as she realized Margie probably assumed she was just as prejudiced as their mother had been. "Oh, Margie. I'm sorry."

"Don't say it like you feel sorry *for* me. I'm happy, Elle. Honestly."

Eleanor felt a smile grow on her face that probably mirrored the one on Margie's. She'd forgotten her sister's nickname for her. Elle. Short, like Margie's preferred name.

"Okay. Well. I'm sorry I didn't ... I wish I had ... Geeze, Margie. Uh, Mags. I'm sorry."

Mags laughed. "Honestly? It just feels good to have told you all of this. Listen, about Mom, I ..."

Eleanor watched Mags struggle with everything she clearly wanted to say. Gorgon had never been able to say he was sorry, either.

"It's okay," Eleanor said. It felt wrong to say it, though. It wasn't okay, not really. It had been so hard to do it all alone.

Mags stepped forward and took Eleanor's hands in hers, looking her sister in the eye.

"I'm sorry. And thank you," Mags said, squeezing Eleanor's hands in a firm, but comforting, grip.

Eleanor smiled at the woman her twin had become, seeing there a reflection of the girl she had loved.

ᛜ

Eleanor stood in the noisy, big-city train station, nervously waiting. It wasn't long before she saw her sister striding through the mass of people, clad in a black leather jacket that somehow looked more trendy than tough. "Mags!"

Mags was breathless as she took her sister's hand. "Elle! Come on, let's get out of the crowd." Eleanor followed, her backpack bouncing as she jogged to catch up. Outside, leaning against a VW bug, was a large, smiling woman in a colorful dress. She looked every bit as cool as Mags with her long, curly hair and big hoop earrings, just in a different way. She was six inches taller than anyone else and had to be Cat, her sister-in-law. Eleanor liked her right away as the woman gave her a warm handshake and then a light hug.

"Girl, what is in your backpack?" It had clunked during their hug.

"Ah. I thought we might find time for a game." Eleanor said, and fished out Mirror Labyrinth.

Mags started laughing and couldn't stop. Cat said, "Oh! An old goldie! Who were you?"

Eleanor twirled in place and cast an imaginary spell with an invisible wand.

"You're a sorceress," Cat laughed. "We are going to have so much fun."

Eleanor looked at Mags, who was shaking her head, but smiling. They wasted no time climbing into the car, Cat telling Eleanor non-stop about the city, the game store, her and Mags's life together. She buckled her seatbelt and rolled down her window. She was who she was, and her sister was who she was, and Eleanor was looking forward to getting to know her sister better than ever.

Karen Menzel (née Bovenmyer) has been playing *Dungeons & Dragons* since 1985, when she bought a copy of the rulebook at a garage sale using her fifth-grade allowance. Her sister's boyfriend left a copy of Dragon Magazine at their house featuring an advertisement for something called GEN CON, a celebration of all things gaming. Karen has attended since 1996, and piling into a van full of college kids to make the journey is a yearly event. Karen teaches and mentors writers at Iowa State University, and has been publishing books, stories, video game scripts, and poems since 2011. Currently, she is writing for Alderac Entertainment Group (AEG)'s new *Ascent of Dragons* game.

Painted World of Witch and Wizard

AKIS LINARDOS

In my world of acrylic forests and pastel towns, only your friendship shone bright colors in my life.

The amethyst letters I painted suspend in the air, then slowly fade. I stand at the edge of a cliff, beside my hut and, on the horizon, miles away from dry land, a framed canvas floats above the sea.

Within the frame, the witch, Feylan, presses their hands against the paned glass separating their world from mine. They'd never touched it before from their black-and-white world. It was forbidden to touch the painting exhibits of the Gallery Tower—which is what I am from Feylan's perspective—Flyn, a wizard in a painting, who once died in a life he can't remember.

Feylan's eyes shift from jade to sapphire and their hair from long blonde to auburn and pixie-short. In this form, Feylan looks like me, a twin from another world.

Inky blood slips their lip but, before it drips, Feylan collects it with a thumb and flicks it. The droplets transform into scarlet butterflies. Feylan whispers, and their words are carried by the cold wind.

"I'm breaking apart. I wish I could tell you everything. I'm a fragmented witch. Because my gray world despised magic, despised the

many colors I dreamed of. Despised my shifting form. I tried to make myself concrete, only to rush my own demise. A flower shouldn't bloom into a rock. A river shouldn't freeze before the storm."

I dip my brush into the bucket and paint mid-air words. *I don't understand. What is happening to you?*

They ignore my question. *"A dance is coming. The Wondrous White. Only happens once every fifteen years in the Gallery Tower. I wish you could come into the Gray, if only to see it."*

How can I help you? What can I do to stop this?

"Nothing. I'm grateful for the conversations we had, through our divided worlds."

My brush trails squiggly letters now, but before I can form a sentence, I freeze staring at Feylan's receding form. The chilly wind carries their final word.

"Be happy, Flyn. You colorful wizard."

My fist clenches around the paintbrush. Why did I not admit it? Why did I hesitate to paint the sentence: *yes, there is a way*?

I was always afraid to step into a world without color. Afraid to ask permission.

Afraid to request a Right of Crossing from the Paintmaster.

The Paintmaster's chamber is large enough to house a giant, and his throne is elevated on a pedestal three times my height. He emanates a scent of turpentine and linseed oil. He's a tall, bearded figure clad in a robe so red it bleeds sanguine colors on his throne, and his golden eyes are daggers pointed at my chest. "Wondrous White? I'm not familiar with this ritual."

"It happens only once every fifteen years," I say, "bringing enchanters from across the country to the Gallery Tower. They conjure white flames and dark bridges to dance upon. It lacks the color of our world, yes, but it bears significance to us."

"And why is that?"

"In the absence of color, they have mastered shapes. We can learn how to use movement and ideas to make our own celebrations even more grandiose. Just think of how the children will see flames flicker with wild tendrils, the peak of colorless beauty, a seed of potential to be elevated further. And in turn, the children will paint over those shapes in a combined celebration of the Gray and the Painted—"

The Paintmaster waves a hand. "Get to the point, wizard."

I bow. "Can you let me enter the Gray, Paintmaster, for this one night?"

He stays silent for a long time, eyes shifting between all the shades of blue. "The Vayani celebration will take place soon. Here. In *our* world."

"I know, si—"

"You prioritize a celebration of the Colorless over your own?"

"No, sire. It's just. I—This—" My throat tightens. All the words I've prepared abandon me. His throne is raised so high; his glare is paralyzing.

"You have grown enamored, Flyn. As a drop of black on a bucketful of white paint, your mind is darkened by visions of things that are not supposed to be yours. By the decree of the divine colors, they are not yours. The Gray is a world we're forbidden from entering but for one reason."

My lips tremble. I know the reason all too well. The world of the Painted is born of the Colorless. We are links of the same chain, drawn by their brush, colored by their magic. Hosts of their souls once they pass on from the Gray. A heaven for their dead.

"Vayani celebrates our connection to the Colorless. If I understand their world better, I would bring bits of the culture back. Inform our celebration further on where we come from."

He leans back in his chair again. My argument makes sense—I know it does.

He strokes his beard. "No."

"Paintmaster, please!"

"There's a point to the segregation of worlds. We are their afterlife, and barring severe circumstances, we won't be breaking the canvas separating us. I won't grant you the Right of Crossing. You had your say—now go."

This is my severe circumstance. I won't be denied this. None of us have memories from the Gray without someone to grieve for us, and my soul has no family to remember me. I am a void vessel, with no one to mourn whoever I was in the Gray, before becoming a Painted. Only Feylan connects me to that world.

Gritting my teeth, I shove my hand into my own skull, my fingers dipping into rippling brain colors.

The Paintmaster stands. "What are you doing?"

"Touching mind, Paintmaster, and I find myself incomplete.

I have to go to the Gray to meet a dying friend. Otherwise, I feel this void within me will only grow until it swallows me whole."

"You be*friended* a Colorless?"

The gushing blood-color of his robes now trickles down the staircase leading up his throne. If he decides to execute me and scatter my colors to the sea, so be it. I have no regrets.

After a long silence, he sighs. "Take your Right of Crossing, then. I expect contributions from you on *next* year's Vayani celebration sevenfold. You will share what you have learned about the gray traditions and how they use shapes for lack of color. I suppose some unfamiliar theatrics might engage the children."

I release my hand from my chest, and the darkness sipping out slowly retreats. "Thank you, sire. May your colors shine brighter than the morning sun."

"However," he raises his hand. "You will paint your own way between worlds, using *only* black paint."

I want to object, but I don't. They need all the other colors for the celebration. I bow my head again in gratitude and leave the royal chambers. I need to begin. The Dance is in three days, and the window is far away and raised high above the waters.

I barely have any black paint for a sturdy sea-spanning bridge, but I'll gather it. And if I have to, I'll even use the color of my own shadow.

ᒎ

Spiders, ants, and dung beetles. My membranous, conjured net envelops all the blackened creatures of the pastel forest. From larval blood and insect chitin, from the fur of rats skittering through boreholes dark.

"Dissolve," my voice thunders across acrylic elms. "Dissolve, collide, and merge. Conjure blackness of clay earth. Conjure darkness of pure sleep."

The creatures blend, and their souls rain down onto the earth to become flowers and animals anew. In a swirling tornado of shadowy strands, their darkest shades funnel into my buckets, filling it with glistening ink.

"Dissolve and become the essence for my bridge."

I sketch a black dock between the cliffs of my home and the sea. Good clean strokes. W-shaped braces to support the structure. Pillars into the foaming sapphire waters to stabilize. The platform takes shape, inclined upwards toward the window on the horizon—miles away. The structure braces to the onslaught of the wind and waves, but it's progressing so slowly that I'm on the second day and barely covered a quarter of the distance.

The ink smells of wet mud and acrylic beasts and insects.

Through the window hovering in the painted sky, the gallery tower of the Gray bustles with activity—the denizens of the painted world framed along the walls of its balconies. Depending on the floor, it could take a whole day to scale it down. But my painting, connected to my mind, gives me glimpses of the ground floor. That's where the festivities will take place.

Five, ten, twenty hours pass.

My mind is pounding with a headache. Has pounded for days now with visions of Feylan sick in bed, visions of them burning away like a statue made of paper tossed to the flames.

Less than a day until Wondrous White. More than a quarter of the distance left to cover. Why did I not put in the request sooner? Why did fear of the Paintmaster seize me for so long?

What if I don't make it in time now?

Never mind clean strokes. I pull out my second brush, dip it into the bucket of black paint, and use both hands. Not pretty, but I can worry about erasing it afterwards.

The window shows a shaky picture, like the whole Gallery Tower is moving. Patrons and candelabras shifting upside down. What are they doing?

I quit drawing Ws and pillars. With haphazard strokes, the platform is now a clutter of gritty smudges. As I move back and forth to dip my brushes into the bucket, I almost trip over the jutting lines of my own making, twice.

Lacking support, the bridge sags under my weight, taking me further away from the window.

I snatch the scissors and cut the lines joining the bridge to the cliff.

Five, ten, twenty lines. With a snap and a rumble, the bridge swivels free of the painted land, supported only by the pillars below. I snip some pillars, discard my shoes, and I sprint along the moving bridge, black paint wetting my bare feet.

The bridge follows my momentum and swivels closer to the window. I reach the haphazard lines—an unstable plank that oscillates up and down. The world stops shaking on the other side of the window, but there's still . . . something off.

I reach the end and, with a leap, I land on the edge of the bridge. The plank propels me upward. And by the time I reach the window, I realize what's wrong.

They've moved my painting to another floor.

༄

It's colder in the Gray.

As I emerge on the balcony of the Gallery Tower, my colors sharpen, my body becomes heavy and rigid, and a rush of lavender-scented air envelops me. The first thing I see is an endless white stairwell stretching both upward and downward, shining against the black walls. The first thing I hear is music and fireworks booming from the bottom. Above, the stairwell fades into starlit darkness. A towering structure to house the countless enchanted paintings—countless windows into our world.

Behind me, there's a painting of my home, my hut at the cliff's edge. Below, moving figures dance on transient black ribbons that melt as soon as they materialize between bursts of bone-white flame.

I dash down the staircase, past paintings of people I recognize—their color in stark contrast to this black-and-white world. Now Aurelia, with her long blonde braid, staring at an orange sky. Now Sorus, in his red hood, fingers gently stroking his double bass. How odd they look to me from this side. Paintings inanimate and unreal.

I pass a thousand steps, but the endless floors still stretch downward. With a thousand more, each of my heartbeats counts down another second wasted.

What if Feylan is already gone?

I finally reach a floor where people dance around me, and I feel their gaze linger on me. I catch my own reflection on a mirror—a man whose color stands out from the rest, no imperfection on his pale skin, his hair a pixie-short and fiery auburn.

The patrons twirl on the balcony with fluttering black robes and white gloves. Where is *Feylan*?

I've memorized their every move, their every smile and mannerism. They were the gestures I've seen in my own mirrors. In my reflection, Feylan's reflection but for the subtle masculine features of my face.

I've learned their gait after witnessing them walking away from my painting countless times. A glance would be enough to recognize them. If only there were a vantage point from where I could see everyone . . .

I rifle through my pockets. My brush. It's still there.

I step over the balustrade to the surprised gasps of those near me. My fingers dangle over the edge. I rub the brush against my feet, suffuse its strands with black pigment the bridge left on my skin. I'm no longer in the painted world, but I command the dual colors of this one, too.

I take pigment from my coat, my pants. Not enough for a bridge. But maybe a rope across?

I make a vertical slice as a fencing master would, and a thin line stretches from my edge of the balcony to that opposite me.

Maybe I'll splatter on the ground floor in an array of colors. But, just maybe, I won't.

I tiptoe along the rope. The heat of white flame bursts rises around me among black ribbons.

Where is Feylan? Where—

Slip. I catch and hang on my fingers. My brush drops to the ground. The rope sags. Everyone turns to me, and finally—

I find Feylan. Eyes cloud-white, and hair long and dark.

Snap.

I'm falling. Amidst a chorus of gasps, Feylan rushes through the crowd, holding the brush I dropped. With lightning-fast movements, Feylan draws a large circle on the floor with crescents along its rim. A trampoline.

With a bounce off Feylan's creation, I land on my feet.

Dazed, I stand still and gasping. Then I spread my arms pretending it was all planned. A clamor of cheers erupts.

Feylan's dimple-cheeked smile perfectly mirrors my own, and their eyes shine, shifting blue colors amidst this world of black and white.

No longer barred by sea and worldly dimensions, we sit side by side on a bench and talk for hours. Feeling Feylan's presence so close is outlandish.

And yet all too familiar.

I speak of Vayani, the festival celebrating our connection to Feylan's world and segregation from it. I share my ideas about how

I will light up the painted skies during Vayani, with shapes learned from Feylan's world. I talk about the bridge I built to reach here. And although Feylan smiles, their eyes are glazed.

"I'll miss you," I say. "You will always be my best friend."

Feylan smiles, the kind of bittersweet smile that exists only to hold the tears at bay. "Maybe I should not—" A spasming cough. Feylan's hair elongates, shifts from black to purple, and their body shrivels so that they are half a head smaller. Their palms are cupped over their mouth, and as I leap to hoist them up, I see the slime spilling out from their fingers. Strawberry scents, and the sludge turns to lady bugs that crawl all over Feylan's arms.

When they raise their gaze, Feylan's face remains unchanged. "Maybe I should not have let the world bend me. Maybe if I didn't let society get into my head. Then I wouldn't have been fragmented. Breaking apart as I am. But it is what it is. Eventually, you have to say goodbye again."

"How can you say *again*?" I ask. "We never really had a *now* but the distant whispers between worlds."

Feylan shakes their head. "We were once one. You and me."

"One?"

"Our magic, Flyn, passes souls of the dead into your world, so they may have a new life—one with color. A life they couldn't have here.

"But you are different. Shamed by my own peers and father, I made a foolish decision. I tore a piece from my own soul and locked it into a painting. Because Father decreed a sorcerer should only have one form. Witch or Wizard. Pick one." Feylan grabs my hand. "You're a part of *me*, Flyn. I *painted* you to house that part of my soul everyone refused."

Feylan's hand is warm in mine. I find myself empty of words.

"I never expected you to enter our world again," Feylan continues. "This is more than I could ever wish for."

My hand clings to Feylan as my tongue still struggles to find words. But before I can say anything, my hand passes through theirs as if they were a ghost.

As if I were a ghost.

"We are one," I whisper.

I taste something metallic and wet spilling from between my teeth. But before I can touch my lips, a force hoists me from the ground and yanks me far from Feylan.

Still reaching for their hand, I'm carried far above the balconies, through the frame that took me here. Then my window to the gray world closes once more. Forever.

Feylan stopped visiting my painting after that night.

A year after the dance, the painted world is festooned with pastel roses fragrant of floral scents and turpentine. The snapping-rope-and-trampoline gimmick has been loved by Painted kids and adults alike, and even the Paintmaster is pleased with my contribution.

Cowled in his red hood, Sorus tiptoes along the rope's length, fifty feet above the town's square. "Is this right?"

"No, not like that," I yell back. "You have to look at your

audience. As if you're really looking for someone among their numbers and you have to find them. Think that you will die if you won't find them."

He looks around, fixates on Aurelia, whose hands are cupped as if in prayer, her long blonde braid let loose.

Slip. Sorus tosses the brush to Aurelia, who paints the trampoline. He drops and after he lands with feigned flair, the crowd cheers and I smile. I wonder who they were in the Gray, if they were together as Colorless before becoming Painted.

I glimpse over my shoulder, to the window beyond the horizon. To the other world. To the empty, dusty floors of the Gallery Tower.

Perhaps it's better like this.

As my gaze drifts back to the crowd of Painted, my thoughts are disrupted. Among the crowd walks my own reflection in female form. Long black hair, shifting amethyst eyes.

Is it true, or merely a trick of the light?

"How?" I ask when the witch reaches me. "How did you enter the painted world? Did you—?"

"Feylan is alive. They painted me. Imparted a segment of their many souls into me. I am their creation and part of them. As you are. My name is Felana. Their female shape."

"Felana..."

"Feylan told me what we once were. When we were *them*. But there are many things I do not know."

I take Felana's hand. Hands that once were one, then split and fragmented between worlds, finally together again. No longer the same.

"I'm not what Feylan was when they painted me," I say. "You'll see you won't be the same as when you were first painted. Part of the same, but ever evolving. 'Motion and flow' is the decree of all worlds, colored or otherwise. So let us be friends, Felana. And grow together from here on out. Feylan's parts once split, now Witch and Wizard, together again."

The witch smiles. "I like that."

The drumming of a tambourine taps through the air, joined by the playful notes of a guitar. The festivities move on, and the Painted gather around the square, dance in pairs, twirl around one another.

I lead Felana into the dance. The scent of sage and sweat surrounds us as she twists in my arms, as she pulls off her hat and throws it in the air, where it breaks into a dozen bluebirds that fly high into the painted skies.

And the world is more colorful than ever.

Akis is a shapeshifter disguised as an AI scientist to steal tech secrets from humans, and maybe help them make their innovations less dystopian for everyone. When his mission is complete, he will settle forever in his Greek cave where he conjures dark stories, some of which can be found at *Apex, Dread Machine, Flame Tree, Gamut Magazine, Heartlines Spec* and other bloodied places. Friends may visit his lair for more unhinged tales: linktr.ee/akislinardos.

Memento Miri

Daniel Myers

Who are you guys again? Axon Security? Are you from the Toronto offices? Because you don't look like the security guys around here—they're all ex-military. Never seen any of them in tailored suits, either ... Look, I'll tell you everything, even the crazy parts. Sorry, I'm just a bit jumpy.

Just lock the doors first and cover all of the windows. Have you started recording? OK, my name is Miriam MacDonald. I've worked as an EMT for Axon Mining for the past five years. I'm registered with the Yukon Coroner's service and have an Associate's Degree in Mortuary Science from Waterloo. I'm also the de facto coroner in Silverton, since I live there. I'd be the mayor and chief of police too, but they haven't bothered with an election in 20 years.

Why do I live there instead of here? The company town has a population of, what, five hundred? I'd rather live with the other thirty-one people in Silverton; they mostly keep to themselves. I'm good with that. I really don't like people, OK? I didn't like them before I moved up here, and nothing I've seen has made it any better, especially not the stuff that goes on in the company town.

I have seen some strange deaths here though, almost as many

as the normal ones. Some people don't do well this far north but can't or won't move down to Whitehorse or whatever. Like the woman a while back who liked to sit on her roof during thunderstorms, or the guy last year who got drunk and decided kissing a bear would be fun. Their family or neighbors bring the remains to me, and I do the paperwork.

Sometimes, nobody's sure what happened, and those cases are kind of fun. It's a puzzle to be solved. There was only one time when I couldn't figure it out; a guy had poisoned his roommate. If there'd been any outward sign, I might have caught it but, without a real lab, there's no way to know for sure. In that case, they flew the body to BC for a proper autopsy.

I'm glad that creep is gone. The murderer, that is, not the roommate. I could tell by looking at him that ... Sorry, got sidetracked. Back to your questions.

I was just cleaning up for the night when I heard the bell at the front door. I went to check and found Reggie standing just outside. Next to him on the ground was a sheet of plywood he'd been using as a makeshift travois, and on the plywood was something covered with an old, blue tarp.

I kind of like Reggie. He rarely comes into town at all, and never talks much. In fact, I think I heard him say more words that night than he's said in years. This was an exception though, because he'd found a body at the bottom of a ravine on the north edge of his property, and since he didn't like anyone on his land, he decided to bring it into town.

Of course, I had to question Reggie outside because he doesn't like the building we use as a morgue. I don't like it either, but I still go in every day. There's no sense in trying to argue with him though—he'll just get upset and leave. So, I pulled the few details out syllable by syllable.

There were no tracks or vehicles, no signs of struggle, and no objects other than the body. He'd placed it on the plywood in the same position it had been in on the ground. The body had not been there two days earlier, and he hadn't seen or heard anything that would suggest how or when it got there.

What? Yes, I do believe him. It's how his brain works. He pays attention to everything and has an incredible memory. He's also the most honest person I've ever met. Couldn't keep a secret to save his life.

I thanked him and told him I might have more questions later. He helped me move the body to a gurney, so he could take the plywood back, and left without saying another word. Then I wheeled the body inside and started the examination process.

It didn't take long before I had to stop and make a call. There were clear signs of physical trauma. Well, sort of clear. I mean, there was dried blood in a lot of places and possible fractures of the skull, neck, and arms. The way the chest was sunken in, I suspected several broken ribs, as well. I'd have to clean up the body to be sure, but it looked like there were multiple contusions on the face and arms likely from blunt force trauma. What? Sorry, he had lots of bruises from being beaten, maybe with a baseball bat.

Someone had killed this guy after working him over, and given that he was cold and still showed signs of rigor mortis, it had happened sometime last night or the night before.

It took until just after 8 p.m. for me to make all the necessary arrangements. The RCMP were sending someone up to run the investigation, and the YCS were going to fly someone in from British Columbia to do a full autopsy. Neither would get in before noon the next day. Until then, I was to take photos of everything, make notes on temperature and such, and check for anything that would help in ID-ing the victim. Then I was to put the body in the walk-in to keep it from spoiling.

Yeah, I said walk-in. The government isn't going to spring for a real morgue for a town this small. The building used to be a meat processing plant, though it never really got used. It was built just in time for the silver mines shutting down and everyone leaving. Now, instead of beef, it keeps people fresh.

Not for food though. There hasn't been any cannibalism here since the 1800s. At least I hope there hasn't.

Anyway, I'd just hung up with the RCMP when I heard a loud pop, like maybe a book had fallen off a table and hit the floor. I looked around but nothing seemed out of place, so I shrugged it off.

Here's where things started to get . . . well, I was going to say weird, but weird is pretty much normal here. Wrong, here's where things started to get wrong.

I got the camera and took a bunch of pictures, and checked the guy's pockets as I went. The clothes were pretty dirty, but otherwise were in good shape, and looked almost formal. Dark wool pants, linen shirt, and a jacket that was something between a suit jacket and a topcoat. No wallet or keys, and no money other than what might have been a large, antique coin in his right pants pocket. In the left breast pocket of his jacket was a leather-bound journal. I set the coin and journal aside to look at later and started checking for labels.

You know how they always say spies cut all the labels out of their clothing to make it harder for their enemies to identify them? It seems kind of a dumb idea to me because when I couldn't find any labels on this guy, the first thing I did was to identify him as a spy. But from what I could tell, the labels hadn't been cut out. It looked like there had never been any labels in there in the first place.

The clothes and everything were surprisingly clean, given the body had been found outdoors. Well, clean aside from the blood. Part of me wanted so badly to wash and clean everything, but that would have destroyed potential evidence and all, so I just had to work around it. I turned on the recorder and started doing the basic examination … and that's when everything went south in wicker. What? Sorry, went to Hell in a handbasket.

Do you know about lividity? It's also called "liver mortis," but I hate that term. It doesn't have anything to do with the liver. It's a discoloration of the skin on a cadaver caused by gravity pulling the blood to the lowest point—very useful for determining time of death and how the body was positioned. Anyway, when I was looking for labels and such on the corpse's shirt and jacket, I'd seen distinct signs of it on the left side. But once I was concentrating on the body itself, I didn't see any lividity at all.

At first I thought maybe I was just tired and had let myself get tricked by a shadow. I mean, it was pretty late, and all the dried blood kind of made examining the skin difficult. But then there were other things that were … off.

For example, in spite of all the blood, I couldn't find any obvious injuries. Even where there were clear cuts in the clothing, the skin underneath seemed to be undamaged.

What really got me though was when I noticed the corpse wasn't cold enough. I hadn't bothered checking the temperature before because it was pretty clear it had been lying dead outdoors for at least a day. But now it was slightly warm to the touch.

I grabbed the thermometer and checked, and the body was just over 13 degrees. Given how the exam room is essentially a large walk-in cooler, that just shouldn't happen. The glowing numbers on the thermostat by the door read 6 degrees, which is a little high but didn't explain anything. To make things worse, when I looked back down at the corpse, the thermometer ticked up to 14. I stood there trying to remember anything from school that could cause a body to warm up like that, and then the damned thing moved.

It was just a spasm of sorts, but that was far more movement than I like in a corpse, and I might have shouted something very obscene. I think the recorder was still running, so you can check it if you're curious. Then there was another twitch, only just in one leg, and it was followed by a loud pop.

Looking back, I think the hip had been out of its socket and had snapped back in. The earlier sound was probably the same sort of thing. If the story ended there, I'd write it up for some academic journal, but no. I watched for the next fifteen minutes as the corpse's temperature kept rising, and just as it went over 34 degrees, the damned thing's eyes opened. I think the only reason I didn't scream was because I was kind of frozen in confusion. But when he gasped for air, I let out a shriek that made up for it.

Have you ever seen someone resuscitated after drowning? No? Too bad. It looked a lot like that. His initial breaths were ragged and irregular, and I stood there like an idiot doing nothing. I'm not sure what I should have done, really. The place is a morgue, not a hospital. I think there's an automatic defibrillator somewhere in the hallway, but other than that and a nearly used up first aid kit, it's all just stuff to use on dead people. I suppose I could have embalmed him, but that would have been pretty rude.

Don't look at me that way. No, not you; the kid behind the camera. Who should I have called for help? The company medical center was an hour away, and it's closed after eight. I'm the most qualified medical expert for a couple hundred miles ... which is kind of sad, really.

I suppose I could have tried CPR, but the guy had woken up from being frickin' dead. I figured anything I did would be small potatoes after that. OK, I was scared too.

What? No. He was dead before, and then he was alive again. I'm not a doctor but I know what a dead guy looks like. I've probably seen more corpses than the two of you put together. Probably. You're not from Toronto though—your accent's wrong. Not Ottawa either. You cover it up pretty well, but I'll figure it out. I'm really good with accents. Sorry, sidetracked again.

Anyway, I did eventually work up the nerve to check his pulse. It was a bit slow and occasionally skipped but, like the temperature, it steadily approached normal.

I'm going to stop using that word ... "normal." I don't believe in it anymore.

His eyes were still open, but they had that glazed over, thousand-mile stare thing going on. Porch light on but nobody home, ya know? His breathing had also settled down a bit, and his skin seemed to be pinking up. I was trying to think of where I could move him that would be more comfortable than an exam table when he had a massive seizure and died ... again.

I checked to be sure and couldn't find a pulse. I had a moment of trying to decide between getting the AED or starting CPR, but before I could do anything, his whole body shuddered, and he gasped for air ... and died. This started a sequence that went on for about an hour. He'd open his eyes and start trying to breathe, struggle along for a few minutes, and then seize and die. I had no idea what the hell I should do, so I stupidly stood there and did nothing. In a way, that was the most horrifying part of the night, watching this guy as he kept crossing the line. After a while though, I realized the stretches of living were getting longer and the dead parts shorter.

By about 3 a.m., he finally settled on being alive. He was breathing a bit raggedly, but his pulse was strong, and his eyes were open. I got the afghan from the break room sofa to cover him with because he'd started shivering pretty badly. Another half hour later, he seemed to be looking around in confusion and trying to talk. Wherever he'd been, he was back.

I know I talked about working with drowning victims earlier, but the stuff that came next was different. When I lived in Ottawa, one of my friends had a sister with profound cerebral palsy. I helped take care of her when I could—she was a real sweetheart—but it was a lot like that. He was obviously in there but couldn't control his body. It was near total paralysis at first, and slowly ... progressed? That just seems like the wrong word. I suppose "improved" would be more like it. Anyway, he improved bit by bit, and even managed to sit up and drink a little water. That's when he started to talk.

It was an obvious struggle for him at first, but he managed to whisper, "Where!"

"Silverton, in northern Yukon," I said. "You were found out in the woods and may have been in an accident of some kind. Do you remember what happened?"

He shook his head in response, and then forced out, "A ... fffraid."

"Afraid" was a good word for how he looked. I expect that, along with "confused," would pretty much sum up how I'd feel if I woke up in a morgue.

"I didn't find any ID on you. Can't you tell me your name?" The moment I asked, he stopped moving. It was clear he was trying hard to remember and was concerned that he couldn't.

"Cahn remm ... ber ... name. Head ... hrts."

I suppose I should have kept him laying down and such, but they didn't design the slab for comfort, eh? I helped him sit up again, and when I was pretty sure he wouldn't fall over, I told him to just sit there while I found him some clean clothes. There was a box of scrubs in the closet left over from one of my predecessors. It only took a moment to get them but, when I got back, he was standing unsteadily by the table and looking like he was ready to hit the floor.

"Where do you think you're going, Skippy?" I asked him. The question stopped him cold.

"Looking for some . . . one . . . I think. Or some . . . thing?" His confusion showed plainly on his face. Given how quickly his speech was getting better, I had the feeling his memory could snap back at any moment. I helped him over to a chair and started cleaning him up.

Yeah, I know. I'm sure it counts as destruction of evidence or something. Sue me. I was dealing with an ex-corpse who was wearing dirty, torn clothes and was covered in dried blood. Rational thought had already abandoned me, and I was running on nothing but instinct and adrenaline. I got a bunch of wet towels and washed off the blood as best I could, and got him into clean clothes. By the end of the process, he was actually able to help a bit.

"Can you tell me your name?" I asked.

He scowled and shook his head. "No. It . . . I . . . no."

"What about why you are in this part of the country?"

"I think . . . looking? No . . . maybe hunting?"

"Huh. You didn't have any hunting gear when you were found," I said. "Oh! maybe these will help." I'd remembered the coin and journal. I'd heard that familiar objects can trigger memories. Maybe it's all total BS that only happens in movies, but it was worth a shot. I got them from the table and showed them to him.

He almost looked like he didn't even want to touch them, but after several motionless seconds, he reached for the book.

It was obviously handmade, and had seen a lot of wear and tear. I watched as he slowly leafed through the pages. They were covered in neat handwriting, all clearly written by the same person. The pages were discolored from age and often dog-eared.

"It feels like . . . something I should know," he said. "Like it is there in my . . . head, but I can't find it."

He made a sort of helpless shrug and handed the book back to me. I wasn't about to give up, though. The book was the only decent clue we had. I paged through it hoping to see names or addresses or something, and a long passage of text caught my eye.

"What language even is this?" I had said it out loud to myself without realizing, but he didn't answer.

I thought maybe it might help if he heard it, so I started sounding out the words, *"Memet te thes that kretan te ten skeatukenka."* It sounded a lot like Middle English—I learned it for fun back in high school—but a lot of the words were strange, maybe mixed with bits of other languages. *"Memet te thes"* could be something like "Remember this."

It wasn't strange to him, though. He started reciting the text where I'd stopped, not reading, just staring off into space. *"Komet te onlich tar nokt, et fliet te fir klere. Scapet tesul en derk ese leote other tier, et maht semplet ese kithes ilosten lank."*

What? Oh, yes. Those are the exact words. I remember pretty much anything I read . . . as long as it's interesting. I suppose I'd have done better in school if I'd found calculus interesting. That's not important here, though.

Definitely some German in there. *"Komet te onlich tar nokt"* . . . "They come only at night"? Maybe. I think I could figure out a lot of it given time. He obviously knew what it all meant though, and must have jiggled some lost memories loose because that bit kind of changed him. Um . . . how can I explain it? Let me try it this way.

There's this neat trick that good actors can do where, with just a few small changes in how they stand or talk or their facial expression, they suddenly transform into a different person. He did that, but I don't think it was exactly acting. He seemed to become taller and broader across the shoulders.

His voice changed too, gaining a tone of certainty, and deepening a bit, maybe. His earlier hoarseness and broken speech had been hiding an accent. Something from Europe, maybe, but I couldn't be sure. The only way I can describe it is that he sounded like a French pirate. That sounds kind of funny though and, by that point, he was anything but funny.

"I remember killing the *skeatukenka*," he said. "The others sent them to seek us out."

"Here?" I asked.

The question seemed to annoy him.

"No, long ago," he said. "Now the others must battle us themselves. I fled to gain time to heal, but they will find me. Soon. I remember everything now, and you should run."

"What?"

"This world is ours, not theirs. We have tended it, and it is us who will reap the harvest."

"So we should call someone, right?" I said. "The government? The military?"

He stopped staring off into space and looked directly into my eyes, and I shuddered. I actually, physically shuddered, because his expression wasn't fear or confusion. It was something colder and harder, like indifference or even disdain.

"This world is ours, not yours," he said. "The farmer does not call upon the wheat to defend itself."

Then he smiled and added, "You really should be running."

I'm good at taking advice.

I think he gave me a head start, or maybe he wasn't recovered enough yet. I was past the end of Main Street in less than five minutes and didn't slow down until well after dawn.

So, if I've answered all your questions, I've got one for you. What are my chances of getting out of here alive? No, that's not what I mean; whatever he did in Silverton, I don't think he's coming after me. It's your accents that gave it away. Most of the time, you sound pretty normal but, every now and then, your voice sounds like his. Are the "others" he was talking about going to show up? I know you're like him. Don't even try to deny it. Nothing I've said surprised you except for when I quoted that part of the journal. Something you recognized but didn't expect me to know.

Or ... wait. Are you the "others?" There's that smile. That's probably a bad sign. Someday maybe I'll learn to think before talking, though I doubt it. At least I'll have company when I disappear. The kid running your video camera has been flipping back and forth between disbelief and fear through the whole story.

Would it make things better for me if I mentioned I remember a lot more of the journal? Stuff that seemed to be about doors, or maybe gateways? And all sorts of pictures and diagrams? No, I didn't think so.

Daniel Myers is a database programmer, author, eccentric cook, and food historian. Much to the surprise of his fourth grade classmates, he has not yet built an infernal machine that can instantly turn a person into tapioca pudding. He lives in Ohio with his family and his collection of singing potatoes.

You Need Not Fear

BRANDON CRILLY

TENSION permeated every corner of the artifactuary. Eyal knew she wasn't helping by frantically throwing together her pack, rattling shelves and making the floorboards creak for the younger apprentices to hear, in their closet of a shared room. She didn't have time to worry about them, yet. Or the artifacts she might knock to the ground, even if they were the only income the artifactuary had. Or the tightness in her chest that made it difficult to breathe.

She needed to catch up to their mentor, Lonos. Before it was too late.

From the workroom, Eyal dashed across the kitchen to the exterior stairs and down from their third-floor shop and residence. Tannon's humidity and the noise echoing from the tightly packed buildings around them was nothing compared to her terrified thoughts: Lonos in chains, carted away to the Seated Ones. The other apprentices traded off to workhouses.

Outside, she burst into a run—and made it three steps before someone caught her.

Lonos's gray eyes crinkled below his shaggy, white mane. "Where are you off to, dear child?"

"I . . . you left . . ."

"And I've returned." His lips twisted into a half-smile. "In time for tea, I think. Shall we?"

༄

When Eyal clambered up the wooden ladder to the roof, Lonos was already seated on the edge. Free of the artifactuary's stuffiness, they could see over the shorter, tightly packed buildings around them at the dense jungle beyond Tannon's walls.

A wavering helix of water floated above Lonos's palm.

"You haven't been doing that for long, have you?" she asked. His expression was blank. "Fervadon?"

"Hmm?" He jerked, and the helix plunked onto the roof's edge, most of it dribbling away. He grumbled and dabbed the rest with his cloak while she served their tea.

Each of his tricks was like that—something minor and arguably without use. Eyal had no idea why the Fonts would give Lonos the ability to briefly change the color of his cloak by holding his breath or snap his fingers to create a purple spark, but it didn't matter. A more powerful "gift" would have only made it harder to hide him from the Seated Ones. Any magic, especially one provided by touching the elusive Fonts, was theirs to control.

"You scared me today," she said softly. "Weren't you worried, going to Ruul on your own?"

Lonos harrumphed over his tea. "We needed to come to an arrangement."

The one other person who knew Lonos's secret was their former employer, Lady Ruul. If they hadn't fled after she learned the truth, she would have turned Lonos over in a heartbeat, to secure a place among the Seated Ones. Now she'd crossed an entire continent to Tannon, to demand their help finding something in the jungle—something more valuable than a Font-touched who couldn't defend himself.

And Lonos agreed, but not for everyone's freedom. Just his apprentices. While he went back to work for Ruul, until she turned him in.

"In the time that we worked for her, did she ever break her word?"

Eyal hid her scowl behind her cup. "No."

But that didn't mean *she* needed to. After all, Ruul hadn't struck any deal with her.

This was Eyal's first time journeying past Tannon's border wall, after years receiving artifacts from the reptilian Ucarna-dar, most of whom still lived in the massive jungle to the north. They'd inhabited the region for thousands of years, long past their greatest empire rising and falling, and refused access to anyone but the most useful and trusted outsiders. That included arcanists and scholars—anyone who could help them unlock the properties of the ancient artifacts left behind by their forebears, and the secrets of the Font magic that rippled through the jungle, sometimes unchecked, like they did across the three continents ruled by the Seated Ones. Lonos and his apprentices used to do that sort of work for Ruul, making Tannon an excellent place to hide. For a time.

She knew she should have been keeping a closer eye on their surroundings, even though they had a Ucarna-dar guide. But the too-quiet trees and the huffing of their horses couldn't hold her attention when she was trying to keep Lonos in close proximity and Lady Ruul as far from her as possible.

Ruul hadn't changed much in three years. Hair still jet black and rigidly straight past her shoulders, face creased a little by middle age. Her vivid green eyes still sparkled; Eyal could remember them glimmering with cold malice toward a competitor or flashing with amusement as they sat on her balcony late at night, discussing ridiculous histories over wine. The only things missing were the two signet rings she used to wear on each hand, and her great-grandmother's pendant around her neck.

Same merchant queen. Ruul rarely gave her word, but she never broke it. Which didn't leave Eyal many options.

A hissing giggle erupted behind her. She glanced back at Brughk, their Ucarna-dar guide, who seemed to be laughing at a cloud visible through the leaves. He'd been hunting artifacts since his blue scales were shiny and smooth, and employed them for help with identification. She used to consider him a friend, but she should have known better than to trust anyone long-term. Having a Font-touched in your family made friendship as ephemeral as distant history.

When Eyal twisted forward again, Ruul's horse had replaced Lonos's beside her.

"I like him." Ruul lowered her voice. "Brughk's amusement is a useful balance for you not wanting to talk."

She pulled her horse away, ignoring the look Lonos gave her. The gentle one that said: *You need not fear, child.*

Ruul and Brughk had told them plenty about their destination. One of the many ruins left behind by the Ucarna-dar's ancestors—in this case, one that Brughk hadn't been able to access, since those ancestors loved puzzles even more than they did manipulating Font magic. Except someone else had. Though the Ucarna-dar tried to keep everyone out, smugglers and criminals inevitably snuck through to hide things from the Seated Ones. Or from their former employers; Ruul wouldn't say whom, but another one of her employees had run off, and unlike Eyal and Lonos, who simply wanted safety, this one took something valuable enough that she had come all the way to Tannon to recover it. After tracking the thief down and extracting every scrap of information she could from them.

She tended to get what she wanted.

Ahead, Lonos abruptly stopped his horse, where their trail crested a small hill. The path below curved through a rockier and less tree-laden part of the jungle—and disappeared inside a churning, misshapen tendril of bright, orange light. It looked almost like the midsection of a massive worm, long enough that both ends were far out of sight; somewhere, they would disappear into the earth, only to reemerge tens or hundreds of kilometers away. The section of Font here undulated in place, ready to expand outward at a moment's notice.

Brughk's nervous hissing turned into a quiet cough. "This must be recent. We've charted every Font spike five kilometers north."

Eyal almost didn't hear him over her heart pounding. That was the problem with the Fonts. The Seated Ones tried to control the Font-touched so tightly not simply for power, but because the Fonts were unstable. Their circuitous path moved and shifted, and any creature they touched was changed unpredictably. Lonos learned that the hard way.

"We should go back," she said.

Brughk consulted a scalesheet map, claws flicking across its surface. "Another trail ahead to the left. We can see if that will take us around."

The new trail was about halfway between the crest and the Font. Only a few steps closer, the horses got skittish, forcing her to concentrate on her reins. By the time she heard hooves moving away, Lonos was several meters past the turn, directly toward the light.

She flicked her reins and sped her horse forward, until she could veer in between Lonos and the Font. Goosebumps spread immediately across the back of her neck and arms; if she turned to look, she knew the orange light would be there, a handful of meters away. Waiting for her, like it had waited for Lonos. But she refused to look, instead fixing her attention on her glassy-eyed mentor, as his mouth worked silently beneath his beard.

Eyal had to repeat his name twice to get him to blink and notice her. "Please," she said, unable to keep the tremor from her voice. "We need to go."

"I . . . was just curious." He didn't sound like he believed it.

Eyal half-expected the light to reach out and ensnare them

both, but the Font seemed content to simply roil. With Ruul out of earshot, she said to Lonos, "I'm going to find a way out of this."

His brow furrowed. "My role is to defend you. Not the other way around."

Every lesson he taught her about composure seemed to burn away in a sudden stab of pain and anger somewhere in her solar plexus. "How well have you been doing at that?"

His face fell, but she refused to flinch until he turned his horse around.

They reached their destination around midday: a shallow depression filled with dense ferns and a stone wall set into a steep hill at its back. Ruul's thief supposedly accessed a buried section of the ruin. Lonos and Eyal would get them inside, Ruul would recover her stolen property, and Brughk would make an assessment for a full expedition.

An hour later, Eyal paced the spongy ground, wiping sweat from her brow. She'd left Lonos and Brughk to puzzle over the wall and its Ucarna-dar markings; her mind was more focused on figuring out an escape, even though Ruul never stopped watching.

Lonos made a noise in the back of his throat. "This isn't going to open."

"Excuse me?" Ruul asked.

"I don't believe it was ever meant to." Lonos pointed at some of the characters carved into the wall. "We've translated enough to tell it's a narrative. Nothing declarative. No subtle warnings or instructions."

Brughk's hissing was almost a cackle this time. "It's a story. A marker!"

"And what does that mean, exactly?" Ruul asked, crossing her arms.

"That the entrance your thief used is somewhere else." Lonos gestured at the ferns and shrubs, and the trees ringing the clearing.

Brughk murmured something about aquatic access and spawning grounds and wandered to the edge of the depression. Lonos watched him go, then whispered to Eyal, "Humor me for a moment?"

Against her better judgment, she nodded.

Lonos started to whistle, so low and light that she doubted Brughk could hear it, and the ferns directly in front of him stirred in a faint breeze. The cone of air moved with him as he stepped. Eyal stuck to his elbow, examining the ground until they found it: a stone disc set into the earth. Eyal brushed the dirt away, revealing curling Ucarna-dar script and grooves set evenly around the stone.

Between the three of them—Ruul content to watch, still—they levered it away to reveal a dark shaft leading down into the earth.

༄

At the bottom, their torches revealed a wide, circular room that could have been the spawning ground Brughk mentioned. The old Ucarna-dar examined the moist, dirt walls and poked his snout into a couple patches of what looked like moss, his oil lantern clattering against his side every time he did.

"Leavings," he declared. "From some creature. Likely old."

The ruin was a convoluted collection of narrow corridors and small chambers. Brughk suggested some of their functions, based on layout and Ucarna-dar script on the walls. The cool dampness was almost as uncomfortable as the humidity.

This close to her goal, Ruul had seemingly forgotten Eyal was there, pausing at cross-corridors to discuss directions. Exactly like back in the day, when she started neglecting their balcony chats because of new business deals. Eyal was still brainstorming escape plans when the corridor opened into a larger chamber than they had seen so far. A few dozen meters wide, the walls curving in and out in places. Irregular floor, sloping up and down in a pattern that Brughk couldn't explain.

"We're looking for a metal lockbox," Ruul said. "One meter long."

Eyal grudgingly fanned out with the others. Instead of searching, she waited for Ruul and Brughk to get far enough away that she could grab Lonos and run.

Until he wandered toward a curve in the wall and called her over. "I'd say this is more interesting than some lockbox."

A pile of bones had been packed into a narrow crevice. They were varying sizes, but the coloration looked like Ucarna-dar. Reluctantly, she waved to Brughk, who let out his longest hiss-giggle as he crouched down. Eyal sat down on a flat rock nearby to give him space.

Ruul stepped up. "You've gotten lazy. Shame on you."

"Excuse me?"

She pointed between Eyal's legs, where a flat, metal shape poked out from under the rock. Trying not to look sheepish, Eyal stepped aside, so Ruul could heft the lockbox herself and start working the lock.

Eyal glanced between her and Brughk. Both distracted.

Lonos drifted closer to watch Ruul before she could grab him. There was a click and a loud squeak, and then a slight gasp from her mentor as he scooped a piece of parchment from the lockbox.

"By the gods, how many of these are in there?"

Lonos showed Eyal the parchment. The name and personal details didn't mean much at first, until she reached the bottom: *Contact made*, with a date and location, followed by the notation *F-T*. This was a record of someone who had been Font-touched, including places they might be hiding from the Seated Ones. Every sheet was.

"Prosperity is as fickle as the Fonts. Yours, mine, or anyone's." Ruul rubbed the place where her pendant used to sit. "I can wipe the last years away with this."

Turning over that many magic users to the Seated Ones would practically guarantee Ruul a place among them. Maybe without turning over Lonos, if Eyal could convince her. Except that would mean confining dozens of people to the fate she'd spent three years protecting him from.

She needed to think. Behind her, Brughk paid her no mind, still crouched over the bones.

Staring at the creature that appeared beside him.

It stood a head taller than Brughk, upper body ending in a misshapen lump of pale, sinewy-looking flesh instead of a head. The creature stood on three leg-like appendages, and several more hung from its body, each one sporting protrusions somewhere between fingers and vines. Tiny nodes scattered about its body caught the torchlight, blinking like eyes.

Brughk let out a nervous giggle, drawing the others' attention.

"Wait." Lonos pointed at another creature, near where they entered. A third materialized behind a raised section of ground.

Brughk didn't back away from the one beside him. "Rysarga, our ancestors called these. Shouldn't harm us. They only feed on decomposing flesh."

The rysarga let out a series of low, guttural noises that seemed to rush over each other, like someone speaking too quickly.

"Semi-intelligent, I'm told," Brughk added.

Eyal looked at the bones. She assumed they were ancient, but thanks to the Fonts, there wasn't much living in the jungle. Not many dead animals left lying around to eat.

Ruul reached for the lockbox. "Well, if they're harmless, they probably won't mind . . ."

The rysarga's chatter stopped. In the sudden silence, Brughk giggled.

Which became a choked cry when one of the rysarga's appendages shot up into his throat. It withdrew its arm and simply let him fall.

He needed to be dead for much longer before they would eat.

In the same instant that Ruul drew her sword, Eyal lunged for Lonos—and Lonos snapped his fingers.

Bright purple sparks erupted in front of all three rysarga, flashing one after another in time with the rapid snapping of Lonos's fingers. They reeled backward, trying to protect their eye-like nodes. With a low whistle, Lonos summoned a stronger gust of air than before, forcing the rysarga back.

Ruul's papers went airborne. She cried out and tried to grab them, knocking Lonos aside.

Something thudded behind Eyal before she could get to him. She spun and saw the pale, misshapen form of one of the rysarga, its limbs poised to strike.

A purple spark erupted between them, blinding her as she stumbled back. The uneven ground caught her heel, but Lonos's sure grip caught her and hauled her away. By the time she blinked, red spots still in her vision, they were back in the tunnel, using the torch in Lonos's other hand as a guide. They only made it another few steps before he staggered with a gasp.

Blood soaked the side of his robes. Eyal frantically pushed them aside, apologizing when he grunted in pain. In the torchlight, she couldn't quite see how serious the gash was. She started tearing fabric from the end of his robes.

"You should've stayed away from that thing."

Lonos's eyes narrowed. "Not my role."

The lockbox landed beside them with a metal thud. Ruul backed into the corridor, waving a torch. Brughk's lantern swung from her shoulder.

She glanced at Lonos. "Can he move?"

"I haven't spent my whole life hunched over a workbench."

"Good," Ruul said. She smashed the lantern at her feet,

adding the torch for good measure as the oil and flame spread across the ground. "Apparently, these things don't like fire."

As Ruul turned back, Eyal cracked the lockbox against her jaw, knocking her into the far wall. Ruul crumpled near the flames and didn't rise.

Eyal stood over her for a moment. Then the papers in the lockbox became more fuel for the flames before she hurled it away, to the sound of distant warbling.

ࣷ

They climbed the rope back to the surface carefully, and Eyal tugged it up. Picturing Lonos in chains helped chase away the image of Ruul being burned or consumed by the rysarga.

"What are we doing, child?" The bleeding had stopped, but Lonos's face was gray with pain.

Eyal marched to the horses, where they'd left them at the tree line. "Going back to town. Getting the others and leaving."

"The best outcome was always my capture. The worst is for the Seated Ones to—"

"I don't care!" Eyal rounded on him. "I'm not letting anyone take you."

When Lonos didn't respond, she thought he had finally listened.

Purple sparks erupted in front of her eyes, and she fell back with a cry. She felt Lonos grab her side but didn't realize what he was doing until coarse rope looped around her wrist and yanked her back. Trying to pull away didn't do any good; she'd forgotten how strong Lonos still was. His hazy silhouette came back into focus in time for her to see the other end of the rope that had saved them tied around the nearest tree.

"My foolishness put you in danger for too long," Lonos said softly.

He dropped one of the artifactuary's work knives at her feet.

"Lonos." When he didn't answer, or even look back, she said it again. And again. Screamed it, but he pretended not to hear her, as he carefully mounted his horse and disappeared between the trees.

Her eyes were streaming, and not from the sparks, as she grabbed the knife and started cutting. The knife was too dull, and the rope was too thick, but maybe—

She'd lost track of time when she heard a thump from the shaft. Eyal didn't waste energy glancing back; if one of the rysarga wanted her, she had the knife, and she was so close—

Blood coated the left side of Ruul's face as she loomed. Her perfectly straight hair was singed in two places.

"Do you know what you cost me today?" When Eyal didn't respond, Ruul asked, "Where is he?"

"I don't know."

Ruul snorted and drove her blade through what was left of the rope, then hoisted Eyal to her feet.

As they rode away from the ruin, it didn't matter to Eyal that they were following Lonos together. She had a terrible feeling about where he'd gone, which worsened when she saw his horse at the spot where they changed trails. Lonos's footprints led left.

Eyal stared into the Font's orange light, as though she might be able to see him inside. The worm didn't look satiated, or hungry, or pleased. Like whom it just consumed didn't matter to it at all.

"I could never decide whether Lonos was brilliant or mad," Ruul said coolly. "Our original agreement is obviously void now."

As she turned her horse away, Eyal thought about the other apprentices. Neither Ruul nor the Seated Ones had a reason to bother them now. She imagined that had occurred to Lonos.

And that he expected her to let him go.

"If you're interested, however, I'd be happy to—"

The rest of Ruul's words fell away as Eyal spurred her horse forward. When it reared, refusing to go further, she leapt from the saddle. Hitting the ground drove the air from her lungs, but she was close enough to reach out and let the Font snap a tendril onto her outstretched hand.

Still hungry, then.

As orange light enveloped her, she shut her eyes and thought of Lonos, hoping that would be enough.

Brandon Crilly's IPPY Award-winning fantasy novel *Catalyst* was published in 2022, with a sequel upcoming in 2025. His games writing has been published by The Story Engine, Fat Goblin Games, We Are Legion and elsewhere, and his first indie title, *B.O.A.*, was released this year on DriveThruRPG. Find out more by following him on Instagram or signing up for his newsletter via brandoncrilly.com.

Turnkey

Richard Lee Byers

When I opened the door to the bedroom, the boy's jaw muscles were clenched. The demon was grinding its victim's teeth in hopes of breaking them. I guessed the spirit figured that was the best it could manage now that its host was strapped down on the bed.

"You could chew his lips," I said, "or even bite off his tongue. But it would spoil some of the fun if you couldn't say hurtful things to people, wouldn't it?"

Before somebody restrained the ten-year-old and the thing inside him, the kid gnawed his hands and forearms, and they were bandaged underneath the shackles. That wasn't the only sign of possession, either. The eyes were bloodshot, bugging out like he had a thyroid disease, and aimed in different directions. Plus, the air stank of sulfur, piss, and shit.

The entity looked me over. "Who are you?" it rasped.

"Who are you?" I replied.

I didn't expect a truthful answer. The demon wouldn't make it that easy. But if I could keep it busy talking, it might not do other things. I took the Sharpie out of my pocket and uncapped it.

"Colin," the spirit piped. Its voice was now a child's voice, and the eyes were normal. Give or take the bandages and restraints, it looked like the boy who belonged in this bedroom with its posters of anime and video game characters and the iPad sitting on top of the dresser.

"You're not Colin," I said. "Colin's just the body you parked in." I started drawing the first symbol on the wall to the right of the bed.

"And you're going to cast me out?" The demon was growling again, and the eyes bulged out of their sockets.

"Don't assume."

The spirit studied me. "No dog collar. No cross or stole. You're not a priest."

"No." I kept drawing. "That was Father Rossi. After what you said to him, he won't be back."

The demon snarled a laugh. "I told everyone he loves to be whipped. And he does!"

"If you say so." I finished the first symbol and circled the bed to draw the next on the opposite wall beside a poster of some character with spiky, pink hair and a gigantic sword.

The demon peered at me. "No crucifix or anything holy, but you carry some manner of talisman. You're hard to read."

I shrugged.

"But I can read something!"

I didn't doubt it. You can hide some things, but certain memories, the stuff you can't help dwelling on, stick to your aura no matter how you try to scrub them off.

The demon writhed in the restraints, contorting Colin's body in a way that threatened to pull limbs out of sockets. Like the burst of laughter, it was a display of the fallen angel's glee.

"*You* were possessed!" it crowed.

"By Bazkiel of the Shining Ones," I said.

"He made you strangle your baby sister! After which, you spent twenty-five years in a prison for the criminally insane!"

I shrugged. It was no fun having the demon laugh at me, but it served a purpose. Like I said, I wanted to keep him gloating and taunting as long as possible.

"But the grief and the lost years don't make you holy," the spirit said.

"I know."

"Then you must be crazy to think you can perform an exorcism. Those designs you're drawing ... I don't even recognize them."

I would have been surprised if it had. I whispered the first incantation.

If I only had one symbol drawn, nothing would have happened. But with two, I'd established a feedback loop that brought both to life as they passed power back and forth. Or something like that. I don't really understand how it works, only that it does.

The drawings gave a feeling of depth. It was like they weren't just lines on a flat surface, but holes in the world that made a person look down and down and down. At the same time, it felt like they stuck outward to form 3-D structures that were more solid than anything else. Everything else in the room, including the demon and me, was flimsy as doodles on a scratchpad.

So it was plain I'd worked magic of a sort. But after I finished the incantation, and the demon took another moment to verify that nothing else was happening, it guffawed.

"I'm still here, mortal! I didn't feel even a tiny pull trying to pluck me from my host!"

Well, it wouldn't have. I moved to the section of wall opposite the foot of the bed. I had a symbol on either side of the demon. When I drew the last and most complicated one, they'd make the three points of a triangle with the bed inside.

"Still," the demon continued, "you have a trace of power. What is this? Wicca? Something out of the Kabbalah?"

"Something like that." It wasn't, but I let the entity mull over the possibilities while I worked on the third drawing.

I got some lines down while the demon nattered on, switching from speculations about the ritual to insulting my lack of mojo to laughing about my possession and what happened after. I suspected the mockery wasn't going to last forever, and it didn't. The fallen angel fell silent, and after a moment, when it spoke again, the gravelly voice held a hint of concern.

"I feel . . . something."

"What do you feel?" I kept drawing and resisted the temptation to hurry. If I botched the ritual now, it would all be for nothing.

"It's like something pushing down on me. The magic isn't casting me out. It's trying to hold me in."

Now that the spirit had figured it out, it was pointless to deny it. "That's right."

The demon howled with laughter, but maybe the laugh held a trace of worry.

"Idiot! I took the child's body on purpose. I want to be here!"

"You shouldn't have a problem then." I drew another line.

"Why are you doing this?"

"Well," I said, "you saw. I was possessed. I know how it works. You demons move in, ruin the life of the person you took over and the lives of people around them, maybe end a life or two, and then go on your way. Isn't that about the size of it?"

The entity hesitated. "I suppose."

"But what if you got stuck inside the host? Possession wouldn't be as much fun then, would it?"

"I don't know what you mean."

"Then I'll lay it out for you." I drew another line. I was making progress. "When a demon possesses someone, and even a trained exorcist like Father Rossi can't pull the demon out, the Church has a place where the families can send them. The priests tell the family exorcism will continue there, but really, they've already given up. They just warehouse the possessed people, so they can't hurt anybody else, and they don't do it at some resort, either. The Church doesn't see any reason to make things nice considering that the inmates aren't really people anymore. Anyway, I'm not part of the Church, but I have connections. I can get you in there."

The demon tried to jeer. It wasn't entirely convincing. "Colin's mother and father would never send him to a place like that."

"Of course they would. You're too good at breaking people. First, you take over Colin. Then you tell Mom about Dad's affair and tell Dad that Mom was on the rebound when he proposed, and that's the only reason she said yes. It was all too much. They're getting a divorce, and they'll dispose of you however I tell them to."

"When they come to visit, they'll see what a vile place it is, and they won't let it keep me."

I drew the next line. "They aren't coming to visit. Ever. I'll tell them it's better not to until there's progress, and they'll be glad to have the excuse to stay away. I said they're ready to move on from their old life. That includes you."

The demon laughed. Forced it, I suspected. "Do you think I care about this suffering you're threatening me with? I'm immortal! My host's lifetime is only an instant to me."

I drew another line. I was almost there. "You're assuming the binding ends when Colin dies. It doesn't. You'll still be inside the corpse when it's buried. You'll lie in the dark and the silence and feel yourself rot till the end of time."

The figure on the bed looked and sounded like the old Colin again. "Please! Don't do this! I'm not gone! Everything it feels, I feel, too!"

"I know," I said. "But here's the thing. You demons broke me too. I said I wanted to save Colin, but that was just to get me in here. I don't care about him. I care about hurting you. If he has to suffer, so be it." I drew the final line and started reciting the final spell.

I glimpsed movement from the corner of my eye. I looked around, and the iPad was flying at me and struck me a glancing blow to the forehead. It hurt, but not enough to stop me saying the magic words.

The iPad pulled back for another go. I flailed at it, swatted it, and must have knocked it out of the demon's psychic grip. It banged down on the floor, and I planted my foot on it to keep it from flying up again.

Unfortunately, there were plenty of other makeshift weapons

the entity could use. A chair rose into the air, tilted back, and rushed me legs first to ram them into me like a bull's horns.

Still reciting, I grabbed two of the chair legs and strained to hold the piece of furniture away. Until I was the only one supporting it, and the back end fell to the floor.

The window rattled in its frame. Cracks zigzagged through the pane, and it shattered. The glittering scraps of glass hurtled at me like a horizontal hailstorm.

I turned my face away and raised my arms for extra protection. The pieces of glass pelted and stung me before falling, clinking away.

When I looked around again, the demon had burst out of Colin and was lunging at me. It was a shadow but still recognizable as a fallen angel. The tattered, ruined wings gave it away.

I was off balance from the barrage of glass, and if the demon had struck with its claws, it would have had me. Luckily, it thought it would be more fun to possess me as it had Colin, as Bazkiel had taken me before. It bounced off my protection. The same spell I'd been casting on Colin, I'd cast on myself long ago, and it could lock a demon out as well as it locked one in.

The spirit raised six-inch claws to rip me apart, but now I was ready for it. I twitched my wrist, and the sheath strapped to my forearm popped the spring-loaded cold iron dagger into my hand. I stepped inside the entity's reach and stabbed it in the chest.

The demon shrieked and withered like paper burning in a fire I couldn't see or feel. In a moment, even the ash disappeared.

That left the incantation nearly completed but not quite. It wanted to manifest and pushed me to say the final words.

That would have been a good deal for Colin. For the rest of his life, he'd be as immune to possession as I was.

But the chances that another demon would try to take him were slim. I was a lot more likely to need the magic than he was. I held in the last few words until the urge to say them faded.

Then I went to the bed and freed Colin from the restraints. Shaking, he hugged me, and I patted his back and said, "It's okay. It's okay." I'd always sucked at this part.

When he stopped trembling, he pulled away and asked, "Is it really over?"

"Yeah," I said. "The demon's never coming back."

He thought about that and then wanted to know, "Would you really have locked me in with it forever? And sent me to that place?"

"No." I figured it was what he needed to hear, although maybe I just needed to say it. "But since Father Rossi couldn't pull the demon out of you, I had to scare it and make it want to come out."

"Then my mom and dad aren't really getting a divorce?"

"I hope not," I said, "now that you're back. But if they do, it's not your fault. Everything bad is the demon's fault."

That, he really did need to hear, even if there'd be moments when he'd have trouble believing it.

I sent him downstairs for a reunion with his family. I'd follow in a second to tell them everything really was okay. But I hung back in case my patron wanted to check in.

It did. I felt a presence older than Hell looming behind me. I didn't turn around. I'd seen it once and didn't want to look again.

"That was spell number five," it said in its genial voice. "Only four left."

"I didn't finish," I replied. "I still have five."

It chuckled. "Fair enough. Five more, and then I claim you."

Maybe. Or maybe I'd have a new trick by then. Either way, revenge was worth it.

Richard Lee Byers is the author of well over fifty horror and fantasy books including *The Doom That Came to San Francisco*, *Marvel Legends of Asgard: The Head of Mimir*, *The Things That Crawl*, *The Hep Cats of Ulthar*, *This Sword for Hire*, *Blind God's Bluff*, and the volumes in the *Impostor* series. He may be best known for his Forgotten Realms novels including *Dissolution* and the books in the *Brotherhood of the Griffon* sequence. He's also written scores of short stories, scripted a graphic novel, and contributed content to tabletop and electronic games. *The Plague Knight*, a screenplay he wrote based on his sword-and-sorcery novelette of the same name, will soon be a feature film.

One Kind of Many, Undefined by Them
Jason Sanford

The prince found me shaping a flute beneath my mother oak's outstretched arms. Found me deep in the forbidden forest, far beyond the hardscrabble farms and dirty towns and his father's stone monstrosity of a castle. Found me even though I'd avoided all humans since I fled his presence the week before.

I knew he watched me when the flute I was shaping fell dead in my hands. I'd discovered a new-fallen tree branch this morning and had been reshaping that dying piece of wood. I whispered loving words to her. Said she'd live again. That I'd shape her into a new form, so she'd sing happiness to the world.

But my magic fled before the prince's angry gaze, the half-shaped flute cracking as the wood truly died. My sisters had always warned that the presence of angry men weakened our magic, but this was the first time I'd experienced it.

"Don't stop on my behalf, Kha," the prince said, stepping from behind a nearby tree. "I want to watch you work."

I sat on one of my mother oak's giant roots, the flint dagger sheathed to my thigh within easy reach. I fed power into my mother, causing her branches and leaves to shiver.

In a polite voice I asked, "What may I do for you, my lord?"

"Do? Nothing. I'm merely inspecting my father's forest."

He stepped forward, his fine leather boots and trousers mere playthings not worn by anyone who actually lived in a forest. His red-linen shirt sparkled to an enchantment for good luck and protection. However, it wasn't strong magic because one sleeve had ripped from the briars that loved to snag foolish visitors to these woods.

"Your father may have title to this forest," I said, "but we're hardly his."

"Yes, you made a similar comment when we spoke last."

"I did? How irritating... for you."

He scowled and stepped closer. I'd been visiting my human friend Ella in town when the prince saw me. Like most young women in town, Ella hated the prince. Sometimes Ella whispered of the women who'd been spirited away to his father's castle never to be seen again. Or women who returned but were never the same, such as her older sister.

Whenever I visited town, Ella let me stay in her bed. While tree sisters didn't seek out physical intimacy as frequently as humans, I still enjoyed sharing kisses, touches and much more with Ella.

But men like the prince, they made me want to never leave my forest.

Behind the prince, standing in the gap in the trees, stood a single bodyguard holding a crossbow. Behind the guard stood two horses. The fact that they'd ridden here without the prince's usual retinue left little doubt of their plans.

Stopping before me, the prince picked up the dead flute. He snapped the flute in half and leaned closer. "Your words last time—"

I cut him off as I stood. I'm taller than him—taller than most humans—with long, thin limbs and hands that had once been wood. I looked down and grinned. "Did I hurt your pride? Did your guards laugh?"

His eyes flared. He raised a hand to hit me . . . and stopped. He stared at the trunk of the massive oak behind me.

"How?" he stammered, reaching out to touch the tree's bark. "What?'

He ran his fingers across my sister's face embedded in the bark. He touched her half-formed wooden body. His hands shook, and he stepped back, uncertainty in his eyes.

His mouth opened—maybe to shout for his guard, maybe to ask questions, maybe to finally understand how ignorant he was of the danger here.

I pulled my flint dagger and cut his throat.

The prince fell back, hands at his neck as he gagged. His guard screamed and fired the crossbow, the bolt slamming into the tree trunk as I jumped over the roots and ran to the other side of my mother for protection.

The guard ran closer, boots crunching on the dead leaves and detritus from 500 years of my mother oak's history. The guard yelled "bitch" and "whore" as he leaned over the prince's gurgling body.

Angry men weaken my magic. But blood is more than a match for anger. As the prince's blood soaked into the oak's roots, I fed my magic into my mother, forcing as much of myself into her as I could without dying. Her roots surged from the ground and grabbed the guard, who screamed as they dragged him under.

I heard a song like a throat of dirt and gravel swallowing a raw piece of meat.

I leaned against my mother's trunk and kissed her rough bark. When I walked back around the trunk, the guard and prince were gone. Blood splattered the roots below my sister's half-emerged form.

My sister turned her wood-grown head to see me better. The bark of her left eye winked. The capillaries inside her left-hand fingers waggled in happiness.

I giggled as I patted her half-formed body. Then I collapsed beside my sister's wooden feet and, exhausted, slept until morning.

☙

I should have fed the horses to my mother oak—I was extremely hungry when I woke, and mother could turn blood into life magic for me and my sister. But the horses were innocent. I led them back to the edge of the forest and released them. I then swept the horse tracks from the forest with a pine bough and prayed to all the trees that the prince hadn't told anyone where he'd gone.

I shouldn't have visited Ella in town last week. I should have ignored the prince when he grabbed my arm and said he'd never been with a woman with skin as brown as wood.

The strongest trees bend when the winds and storms howl. Because of that they rarely break.

I refused to bend. And now me and my sister might pay for such hubris.

But my sister couldn't yet leave our mother's trunk, so I'd

have to deal with whatever trouble came. I found another freshly fallen branch and began shaping a new flute. I also listened to the distant trees in the forest buzz about the king's guards searching for their prince. So far they only searched near the forest's edge where the horses had been found.

Under my fingers the branch flowed and reshaped, spinning into new dreams of music and air and happiness. I remembered my older sisters reshaping wood into toys and beds and chairs and even our hut when I was young. I had a long way to go before I reached their levels of power, but I still loved my little flutes.

Taking a break, I pricked my finger with my dagger and touched the blood to my sister. She smiled, the blood enabling her to free a little more of her body from the wood.

I was nearly finished with the flute when a male voice called out to me.

"Kha, you there? May I approach?"

"You angry or upset?" I yelled back. Angry men may kill magic, but not all men were angry. At least not all of the time.

"I'm actually quite happy. Thanks for asking."

A middle-aged man in hunting clothes stepped from the trees. His name was Tapao, and he stood tall and lanky, with a brown beard speckled white as if snow forever fell from his face. He was the king's huntsman and had known my older sisters long before I was born.

Tapao stopped a good fifteen yards from me and my mother. While Tapao liked me, he was also a careful huntsman familiar with the dangers of this forest. He knew even if I dumped most of my power into my mother's roots, at this distance the roots were thin and weak and couldn't pull him under.

He watched as I finished molding the branch, opening the final holes for fingers. I sighed as an almost religious ecstasy flowed through me into the brand-new flute. I raised the mouthpiece to my lips and blew. Haunting music floated across the glade.

"Nice flute," Tapao said. "Spooky too. Makes the hairs jump right off my neck."

"Will you take care of her?" I asked. He nodded and I tossed him the flute.

"Thanks. I'll give her to my granddaughter. How are your older sisters?"

"Haven't seen them since they wandered off."

I didn't ask why he was here because I knew. Tapao pulled the bow from his back and laid it on the ground along with his short sword. He pulled a leather wine skin from his backpack and offered me a sip. I shook my head, not wanting to leave the oak's protection. I fed a touch of magic into mother just in case.

"I see you're growing a new sister," he said. "If I dug into the ground under your mother's branches, would I find the missing prince and his guard?"

The oak's roots shivered, causing Tapao to step back several paces, putting him further away from his weapons on the ground. I sighed. If he could be so trusting, I'd do the same. I walked from my mother's protection into my hut, where I carried out two chairs. We sat and sipped his wine.

"The prince tracked me here," I said. "He saw me in town and wanted my body, but I refused. So, he and a guard came to hurt me."

"He was a pompous ass, just like his father," Tapao said. "And like his father he hurt women. I won't miss him."

Tapao drank from the wine skin again before offering me the last swallow.

"However," he continued, "the king won't stop until he finds his son. You hid his path well, but I was still able to track him here."

I pointed to the ground in front of my sister. "The bodies are under there. Won't be much to them but bones in a few more days."

Tapao waved at my sister in the tree. She waved back.

"I remember when your older sisters created you," he said. "They were lonely, so they used their magic to pull you from your mother's embrace."

I looked away, not wanting Tapao to see my eyes water. Loneliness. That's why I'd done the same, empowering mother to create a new sister. Loneliness was also why I wandered into town to trade my flutes and visit Ella.

I just wanted to be me. But I also needed to be around others. Why couldn't those two needs live together?

"I won't tell anyone I tracked the prince here," Tapao said. "But the king's enchanter, that's another story. He's been away on business and returns tomorrow. Once he arrives, he'll find you."

I remembered the enchantment in the prince's shirt, which now rested underground with the rest of his body. A good enchanter would locate that shirt and the body that once wore it.

"Will the enchanter come here alone?" I asked.

"No. Once the enchanter locates the prince, an army of men will march here. I suggest you flee."

"I can't leave my sister."

"How long until she emerges?"

"Maybe three days. The prince and his guard were kind enough to feed mother a fair amount of blood, which sped things up."

"Not soon enough." He glanced again at my sister. "May I feed her?"

I nodded.

Tapao stepped toward my sister, who smiled. Tapao smiled back as he slit his palm with his short sword. He held his bleeding hand to my sister's forehead.

My sister pulled a little more of herself out of the tree, freeing her body enough that she could swallow air with her lungs and laugh. Tapao wrapped his hand with a cloth as he walked from the tree.

"I'm glad you're no longer alone," he said. "But the enchanter will find you tomorrow. If you won't run, there's only one way to keep your sister safe—you must buy her enough time to emerge."

Tapao held up the flute I'd created and blew a mournful note before placing it in his pocket. He then hiked back toward the world of men.

༄

That night, I snuck to the forest's edge, near enough that I could see the candles and torches in town. Normally, I'd go to Ella's house near the town's center, but I saw the king's guard patrolling the streets. Instead, I sat under a small oak tree and watched the town until I heard a haunting tune echoing through the night. I ran through the trees until I found a woman standing on a moonlit path. She stood in the dark blowing a flute I'd crafted, the music shivering my face into a big smile.

Ella.

We hugged, her head barely reaching my chest as she cried. I held her until she calmed down, happy to hold her in my arms again.

"I thought that bastard killed you," she whispered. "He bragged to all his guards he was going into the forest to find you."

"I'm fine. But he's dead."

"Good," she said as she spat at the ground before hugging me back.

Ella ran a small music store in town. When the prince confronted me outside her store during my last visit, I'd seen the anger and fear in her face—anger at what the prince had done to her older sister along with fear at being unable to protect me against his power.

"You need to leave," she whispered. "They'll find you."

"I will," I lied. "But I may not be able to trade flutes with you for a while. I wanted you to know I care deeply for you."

Ella smiled as she looked up into my eyes. She took my hand, her flesh pale against the brown of my own. She bowed slightly and kissed my long fingers, causing my skin to shiver with delight.

"My lady," she said with a laugh, "you do not need to explain yourself. Just keep yourself safe."

I laughed and kissed her before running back to my sister.

⁓

The next morning my sister breathed on her own with one leg completely free of our mother.

I told her to remain quiet. To not move if the king's guards found her. Maybe they'd overlook her. Think of her as merely a strange carving. I told her that once she was completely free of the oak, she must flee deeper into the forest.

She grabbed my arm with her one free hand. Tried to tell me not to do this. But her vocal cords were too weak to speak more than the faintest of whispers. If the enchanter found her before she was free, he'd kill her. Or she'd use so much of her power defending herself that she'd still die.

I cut my palm and fed my sister as much blood as I could spare. I asked our mother to give me the prince's enchanted shirt. She shook her leaves in irritation—gifts were not supposed to be returned—but in the end she agreed because she loved me deeply. While she'd never give up the nourishment of the prince's half-digested body, a shirt was a minor thing. Her roots ripped the shirt off the prince and raised it above the dirt and gravel.

After thanking our mother and kissing my sister, I walked toward the forest's edge.

⁓

I found Tapao sitting on a fallen tree. I tossed him the prince's shirt, which he tucked into his belt.

"I must bind your hands," he said nervously, holding up a length of rope. "Otherwise, the king will suspect me."

Even though I'd known this would happen, I reached out in panic to a tree next to me. The tree swelled to my magic, its limbs hissing and its roots quaking underground like dangerous snakes waiting to bite.

"I'd prefer to do this without being killed," Tapao added. "And it's hemp rope, not iron."

I eased back my magic, calming the tree. I held out my hands, and Tapao bound them.

"Make sure you're there when my sister emerges," I said. "She'll want to save me. Tell her to flee deep into the forest where no one will find her."

Tapao nodded.

When we left the forest, we found the king and his guards arrayed in all their battle finery in an open field. The king sat on his horse while the guards stood in ranks holding swords and spears. Between them and the forest stood the enchanter, whose fingers hurled dazzling colors and loud explosions into the sky.

"The enchanter loves this peacockery," Tapao muttered. "Gets the troops excited. Makes the king believe the fool's magic is powerful."

We stepped from the trees and walked toward the king.

The king and his guards stared in shock, but the enchanter didn't see us because he faced the wrong way. He chanted incantations and waved his wooden staff, rainbows shimmering in the air above him. The king tried to subtly catch the enchanter's attention, but the man was absorbed in his own performance.

Losing patience, the king rode his horse forward, forcing the enchanter to jump aside to avoid being trampled.

"Your majesty?" the enchanter asked.

"Look, you fool," the king bellowed.

The enchanter turned. He was a tall, thin man with a long white beard. He wore a black robe flickering with embroidered images of dragons flying across starry nights. He held a wooden staff nearly as tall as me.

He also looked shocked by my sudden appearance, as if I'd upset his carefully managed plans.

Tapao held up my bound hands and stopped a few yards from the king, where the huntsman bowed. "Your majesty. I've captured the woman who killed our beloved prince."

The king froze. "He's dead?" He glared at the enchanter. "You said he wasn't dead."

"The runes promised he still lived...," the enchanter muttered.

Tapao pulled the prince's shirt from his belt and tossed it to the enchanter. The shirt's red linen showed the darker reds of dried blood.

"She had this on her," Tapao said. "I can't find the prince's body, but she admitted killing him and his guard."

"Well?" the king demanded.

The enchanter danced his fingers over the shirt. "It's his shirt, your majesty. And his blood."

"Take her to the dungeon!" the king yelled as several guards rushed forward to grab me.

"Wait, your majesty," the enchanter said, stepping before me and staring up at my face. "She's magic. She might be dangerous."

"What do you recommend?"

"Imprison her in my laboratory. Let me study her. I'll make her tell us where the prince's body is hidden."

"Might not be wise, your majesty," I said. "Is this the same man who enchanted the prince's shirt? That magic didn't protect your son."

The enchanter slammed his wooden staff into my head. I would have fallen to my knees except for the guards who held me tight. The world rocked sideways before unconsciousness grabbed me.

But I passed out with a smirk on my face for all these damned men to see.

༼ ༽

I woke in a man-cage crafted from cold iron hanging in the enchanter's laboratory. I touched the iron bars and cursed from the pain, yanking back my hands. I'd seen iron many times but had never before touched it.

The woods of walnut, maple, and oak surrounded me. But they were dead now, cut into the shapes of tables and chairs and bookshelves. Potions bubbled in glass containers alongside mortars and pestles scented by smashed herbs and plants. I tasted the false magic of alchemy and the desire for base metals to turn noble. I smelled only a faint glimmer of real magic hidden among countless good luck charms and other so-called enchantments.

"I'm glad you're awake, my dear," the enchanter said as he stepped around a table holding a large book.

"How long have I been out?"

"Most of the day. You prepared to answer my questions?"

If I'd been unconscious for most of the day, that meant there were still two days before my sister emerged from our mother. Three days to be safe. All I had to do was keep the enchanter from locating the prince's body until then.

"I may have answers," I lied.

"You misheard."

I didn't understand, but the enchanter didn't care. He held his book before my eyes. The pages, created from the shredded remains of dead trees, made me shiver in disgust.

"Ah, you hate dead trees. That confirms what you are." The enchanter pointed to an inked illustration of a woman emerging from a tree. "You are a dryad."

"Never heard that term before."

"It's what you are."

"It's what you're calling me. Nothing more."

The enchanter slammed the book shut. "The king told me his son had been insulted in town by a young woman who looked like you. I now see why the prince sought to teach you a lesson."

"If your enchantments had taught the prince to treat people with kindness, he'd still be alive."

The enchanter grabbed his staff and slammed it into the cage, smashing two of my fingers against the metal. I wanted to scream in anger and pain, but instead yanked my injured hand back and glared.

"I have questions," the enchanter said.

"Ask them."

The enchanter laughed and tapped the top of his staff to his lips, his white beard flowing around the wood like a colorless waterfall. "I have questions," he repeated.

My broken fingers were already healing, even though my magic was weakened. But his questions without questions were frustrating. I wanted to yell. I wanted to take his staff and break the cursed, dead wood it was crafted from.

But as I stared at the enchanter's twisted face, I realized he wasn't going to ask anything. He already believed he knew all the answers he sought. He knew what he wanted me to be. He knew what he wanted to do.

"You will lead me to the prince's body," he whispered. "You will demonstrate to the king the vast powers I wield."

"Those aren't questions."

The enchanter tapped his staff gently against the metal cage. "They will be," he said. "They will be."

Men hurt you.

Men demand answers they don't want to hear.

Men uproot you from life even as they deny doing anything of the sort.

Men are the enchanter, dazzling with lights and sounds and pretending that's all there is to magic and life.

Men are the king, imprisoning you and pretending this proves his power.

Men are Tapao, a huntsman who thinks he knows me but doesn't, and on whom I must rely to save my sister.

Men are the prince, following you home because he can. Knowing he can hurt you. Refusing to accept "no" because he is the prince.

After three days of not asking me any true questions, aside from demanding to know where the prince's body was, the enchanter dragged Ella before me. She was unharmed and unbruised. Unlike me.

She gasped when she saw me in my iron cage. But she couldn't help me. Guards stood on either side of her, pinning her arms.

"We all need music," the enchanter said. "This young lady runs a beautiful store which brings happiness to people across the king's lands. It would be a shame to see her, or her service to our realm, harmed."

I nodded. It had been three days. My sister should be safe.

"I'll show you the prince's body," I said. "I'll make you look powerful. But only if Ella's unharmed and freed."

The guards took Ella away, dragging her back out as she called to me. As Ella begged me to use my magic to free myself.

But I was already free. Even if men like the enchanter or the king didn't realize it.

༒

In the morning, I staggered though the castle gates, my hands bound in iron manacles that burned my skin and an iron chain burning more pain around my waist. The chain led to the enchanter, who tugged me forward like an animal.

I fell to my knees as we walked over the drawbridge. As I touched the dead wood planks, I gasped. Had these trees hurt like me? Had they dreamed of standing tall even as they were cut down?

Irritated, the enchanter ordered two guards to grab my arms and carry me.

"She's too weak," the king said from astride his horse.

"We want her weak, your majesty," the enchanter said. "We are going into her place of power. But the iron stops her. That, and my magic."

We marched across the fields surrounding the castle and past the town—I saw Ella crying among a crowd of watching townsfolk—and into the forest.

I thought being back among the trees would help me, but the iron kept me weak. As we hiked deeper into the forest, I staggered against trees here and there. When I touched them, they rattled and groaned, wood flexing in shock at my pain. But I didn't have enough power left for the trees to save me.

Still, the guards fell quiet when the trees shook. One of the men holding me whispered, "Please forgive us."

"I despise these woods," the king announced. "Our actions today will be the first step toward gaining control of this damn place."

The guards stiffened their backs at his words. I imagined the king's men coming here with axes and saws and fire. My stomach sickened at the thought. And if I died, there would be little the forest could do to stop an attack.

But at least my sister would be safe. Maybe she'd encounter my other sisters and find her own happiness far from the dangers of men.

I was ready to die. Let these men have their prince's body back. Let them kill me.

And those were my thoughts until we reached the mother oak, where Tapao sat on one of my chairs sipping his sack of wine.

A dozen yards away stood my sister, standing beside our mother oak's trunk. She was free but hadn't fled. I started to scream at Tapao. To ask why he hadn't saved her. But my voice caught on the shards of my body's weakness and failed.

The king rode his horse up to Tapao and gazed at the huntsman, who remained sitting. The enchanter approached, puzzled.

"Will you not bow for your king?" the enchanter asked.

Tapao took another sip of wine and pointed toward the oak tree. "The prince's body is buried under that oak," he said, as if the king and his men were merely dead leaves blowing before his eyes.

"How do you know this?" the enchanter asked.

Tapao pointed again to the oak. My sister's skin was still wood and bark, which camouflaged her when she stood still. But now the king and the enchanter saw her. The king, ignoring Tapao's disrespect, urged his horse toward the tree. The enchanter and guards followed.

I struggled against my chains but couldn't break free. "Run!" I yelled, finally finding my voice.

My sister shook her head. She smiled, but it was the angriest smile I'd ever seen.

"What is this thing?" the king asked.

"That . . . is her," the enchanter said, pointing at me. "A copy of her, newborn and without the appearance of human skin. A tree that walks."

The king's horse stepped back from my sister, as if finding her distasteful. The guards holding me tightened their grip, as if only now understanding how truly different I was.

"Take hold of it," the king yelled to several guards. "The rest of you dig for my son."

Run, I thought. *Please. You don't yet have the power to fight and live.*

But my sister didn't run, not even as the guards raced forward and grabbed her. Instead, she fed her power into our mother.

I reached out again with my magic, trying to break the stranglehold the iron had on my body. I cursed. I screamed. But I was too weak.

My sister, though, laughed in anger.

Our mother oak groaned to my sister's power and shook her leaves. The king's horse reared, the king struggling to control him, as the ground quaked from roots rising up to grab ankles and legs.

A guard screamed as he was pulled underground. Other guards hacked with swords at the roots rising around them.

"Stop," I pleaded. "Please. Don't share so much power with our mother. You'll kill yourself."

But my sister didn't listen. Roots grabbed the king's horse

and pulled his rear legs down, throwing the king to the dirt where new roots pulled him under as he shrieked.

The king's disappearance turned the guard's panic into a rout as they fell over one another to escape. My sister giggled as hundreds of roots burst to the surface, dragging down the remaining guards as they begged for their lives.

Only the enchanter remained. In the confusion, he'd snatched my iron chains from the guards and held me against his body, backing both of us away from the mother oak while holding a steel knife to my throat.

"I'll kill her," the enchanter said.

A root grabbed the knife from his hand as others pulled us both underground. The enchanter clung to me like a scared child as dirt and gravel pelted us. He whispered, "Please," before his mouth filled with soil as he screamed, the sound as dull and heavy as boots sinking into deep, wet mud.

The roots pushed me back to the surface. I lay gasping on the ground.

My sister staggered toward me, her legs thin as diseased saplings, her chest quivering with each breath like a rotten tree in a storm. I stood up, but iron still held my arms and waist.

"Free me," I yelled at Tapao. "I have to help her."

Tapao ran forward and jammed his dagger into the manacles' lock, popping it open and unwinding the iron chain. He threw the iron away as my power quickly returned.

But not soon enough. My sister fell beside me, growing thinner and weaker before my eyes as her remaining magic drained away.

"No, no," I whispered as I cried. "No."

I held my sister as she kissed my cheek.

"Thank you," she said.

Then her body finished rotting and she collapsed to dust.

With the iron gone, I grew more powerful. The mother oak shook in fury and roots rose around us.

"You were supposed to save her!" I yelled at Tapao. "You were supposed to tell her to flee!"

Roots grabbed Tapao's arms and legs and pinned him to the ground. But he didn't go under. I wanted to see his face as the roots squeezed him to death. I wanted him to know my anger and pain.

"I tried," Tapao gasped. "Believe me, I tried. Her... choice... her life. She refused to leave you to die."

The roots stopped squeezing. I ran my fingers through the dust which had been my sister.

The roots tossed Tapao toward the hut, where he lay on the ground shaking. He sat up, leaned against the hut, and pulled out his wine sack.

He drank all his wine without a word.

Tapao was right. My sister's life was her own from the moment I created her. She wouldn't sacrifice my life for her freedom.

I stayed in my hut for days, crying and screaming before eventually coming back to myself.

As for Tapao, he returned to the castle with news of what happened to the king and his men. Since then, no one entered the forest, not even Tapao. He didn't trust me. Which is fair, since I did try to kill him. And while I understood he couldn't force my sister to flee, I was still angry at him.

But I did wonder: What did a huntsman do when he was afraid to enter the woods?

I still shaped flutes from fallen branches. Instead of traveling to town, I left them on the edge of the forest, where the townsfolk and farmers found them. And Ella often met me under the trees at night, snuggling against my body until morning came.

She asked me once to come to town and again, share her bed, but I shook my head. She knew enough not to push and merely hugged me close.

The mother oak was still scarred where my sister emerged. A hole shaped like my sister's body. Every morning, I caressed her imprint.

I wished I could have known my sister. The mother oak whispered that my power could create a new sister. That we could still enjoy a life together.

Maybe someday I would.

Maybe someday I would play a flute in town as my newest sister danced. Maybe someday I would mend my friendship with Tapao. Maybe someday no one would care that we were not them. Or they us.

Maybe.

Jason Sanford is an award-winning science fiction and fantasy writer who's also a passionate advocate for fellow authors, creators, and fans, in particular through reporting in his *Genre Grapevine* column (for which he is a four-time finalist for the Hugo Award for Best Fan Writer). He's also published dozens of stories in magazines such as *Asimov's Science Fiction*, *Interzone*, and *Beneath Ceaseless Skies* along with appearances in multiple "year's best" anthologies and *The New Voices of Science Fiction*. His first novel, *Plague Birds*, was a finalist for both the 2022 Nebula Award and the 2022 Philip K. Dick Award. Born and raised in the American South, Jason's previous experience includes work as an archaeologist and as a Peace Corps Volunteer. His website is www.jasonsanford.com.

Eye of the Beholder

Jennifer Brozek and Raven Oak

To *be an icon in an iconic city is to always be a target. Since I came into being, I have been an object to be claimed, marked, photographed, and blamed for an unsatisfactory outcome. I am everything from a background prop in a posed photo to the unwilling witness to countless crimes to an uncaring god of all I survey—even if that isn't much more than the underside of a bridge surrounded by burnt-out floodlights, a paltry plinth with a decades-old brass plaque no one reads, and trash strewn about by admirers, haters, and indifferent tourists in equal measure.*

Once in a while, I become more than that. I become a silent priest to an emotional confession or a sympathetic bartender to one who comes to me for advice. In all cases, my silence keeps the words tumbling from your mouths because all that is needed is my august presence. The rest, you figure out for yourselves.

A fine mist painted the Seattle sunrise gray as Detective Blake stood sipping their coffee. A tech bumped their shoulder, and Fremont's best sloshed out of their cup. "Shit," they muttered, staring at the growing stain on their Seattle PD hoodie. Their glare glanced off the tech as he leaned closer to photograph the body.

Young. White. Poor by the looks of his ragged clothes. Either that or he loved grunge music a bit too much. His body lay beside the stone-covered VW Bug grasped by the troll's left hand. Blood spatter marred the car's rear window while scuff marks on the ground pointed to more than one person.

To the side, an evidence marker noted a discarded spray can, and they stepped behind the Bug where graffiti marred the tail end. *Kay … Kaz …* The particular curve of the "K." Fancy for a tag and more artistic than most achieved with a spray can. The unfinished tag meant little to them, but maybe petty crimes would recognize such talent.

The medical examiner turned away from the body, and they nodded to catch the old man's attention. "Hey, Doc, what're we looking at?"

He pointed a gloved finger at the Bug's rear window. "Point of impact. COD's probably blunt force trauma, but I'll know more once I get the body on the table."

"Looks like a struggle. Any prints?"

"A few. Mostly on the victim's arm. I'll know more—"

"When you get the body on the table. Yeah, yeah. I got it."

Another tech pointed at the ground near the Bug's tire, and they glanced at the dusty concrete. Something had sat there. Recently. They snapped a quick photo with their cell phone.

"Figured you'd get here first, Charlie!"

Detective Blake tensed at their partner's voice, though "partner" was a far stretch, as the man had about as much drive as the VW Bug. They refused to acknowledge him and, instead, stared up at the troll's lone hubcap eye. "You've probably dealt with your fair share of idiots. Any advice?" they muttered.

"Wha?" asked Detective Peters as he leaned over their shoulder. He whistled sharply at the blood-splattered VW Bug. "That's gonna be some detailing job. Say, wasn't this your 'hood growing up?"

They shook their head. "SODO gal."

"That's right. *South* of Downtown. You were poor like our vic, yeah? But *gal*? You ain't exactly the feminine type."

Charlie ignored the jibe and pointed at the mark left in the dust. "Something was taken from the scene. Heavy enough to leave an imprint in the dust here. Two sets of footprints too."

"Yeah, too bad the old man here can't talk. Then we'd know." When he jabbed his finger at the troll, he frowned. "Maybe some neighborhood cameras. You should check. Lotta drug deals go down 'round here. All them college kids and art majors. Didn't you wanna go to art school when you were younger?"

He knew the answer, but it didn't stop him from goading them all the same.

"It could be drugs. Maybe that's what was in whatever was taken." They removed a small tape measure from their jeans pocket and held it over the imprint. "About sixteen inches wide. Backpack maybe? You could be right about those art students."

"Heh. Absolutely. You know, you're more Seattle than I figured, Charlie."

They tucked the tape back in their pocket and ran their fingers through their short blonde hair. "How's that?"

"Artsy, sympathetic, and queer to boot. Maybe you got more

in common with the vic than you know. Let me know when the prelims come in. Might be something the techs caught that you missed."

Peters laughed as he strode in the direction of his buddies—a bunch of street cops who cared more about harassing folks than solving crimes—and they sighed. Fremont was their beat. Their responsibility. They'd be damned if they were going to let a cop like Peters turn this crime into another excuse for why people "like her" shouldn't be on the force.

They glanced up at the Fremont Troll and tipped their coffee cup in his direction. He couldn't talk, but maybe the folks in the neighborhood would.

Would that I could become a monster of old, the troll under the bridge to eat the unwary, the ungrateful, and the callous. I don't care that Peters is a servant of the City. He is no servant of mine and, thus, he would be prey. Conversely, a person I have seen grow up over the years, Blake, is one of mine: a true servant. I do not claim they would not become a meal, but I would not seek them out for retribution.

Three hours later, Detective Blake stood outside a small craftsman home in Burien, a neighborhood near their childhood home. There'd been no cameras at the troll. The Chamber of Commerce had never raised the funds to mount their "Troll Cam," and the neighboring traffic cams had been too far away to see anything. But the victim's prints had been in the system, one Travis Wilson, nineteen, an art student at Cornish School of Arts.

A heavily aged woman in a housecoat answered the door, and her lips trembled when she noted Charlie's badge. "How bad is it?" she asked.

"Detective Blake, Seattle P.D. Are you the parent or guardian of Travis Wilson?"

"I'm his grandmother, Betty. Raised Travis since he was in diapers. You gonna tell me what this about?"

Her eyes pled with Charlie. It was a look known to any cop who took the job seriously. Charlie kept their face on neutral. This one was going to be rough. "Can I come in and speak with you for a moment, ma'am?"

They'd expected Betty to crumble then and there, but the old woman stood up taller as she moved aside to allow Charlie entrance, then gestured for the detective to have a seat on a paisley couch covered in plastic.

"Have you ever known Travis to be involved in any criminal activity?"

Betty turned a sharpened gaze on Charlie. "If you have my grandson's name, then you know about that vandalism charge. They never did seal his records like they promised. Why don't you tell me why you're here, and we'll see if I can't help you?"

This grandmother knew the system well, but then, most people living in poverty did, and not always by choice. Charlie nodded to themself before speaking. "This morning, your grandson was involved in an altercation at the Fremont Troll. He was tagging it when a struggle took place—"

"A struggle with whom?"

"We don't know yet, ma'am, but your grandson was injured in the struggle—"

Betty shot to her feet, moving much faster than anyone that age should move. "Where is he?" she asked as she grabbed a light shawl.

"Ma'am, I regret to inform you that your grandson hit his head in the struggle and died at approximately three this morning . . ." Betty's eyes glazed over as Charlie spoke. They'd found unidentified prints on Travis's arm and, while uniforms had canvassed the neighborhood, no one but a stone troll saw or heard anything. Their phone buzzed and a quick glance showed a sketch of what he'd been tagging—one word. Unis must have arrived at his dorm. "Does the word *Kazza* mean anything to you?"

"No, but then Travis was always doodling all sorts of things. It's why he goes to art school. *Went.*"

Unshed tears pooled in Betty's brown eyes, turning them almost black, and Charlie pulled out a packet of tissues to pass her. The old woman accepted the offering but refused to grieve in front of Charlie.

"Did he have his bag with him? I'd like that, and his sketchbook, back. If you don't mind."

Charlie shook their head. "We didn't find it, but when we do, we'll return it when we can. No one likes this question, but I have to ask: was Travis ever involved in any illegal drugs, ma'am?"

"No. He knew better."

"Are you sure?"

Betty pursed her lips together. "Both his parents were addicts. They died from the needle. There weren't any way he was involved in that junk. Now, if you don't mind, I need a little time to myself."

A clear dismissal and one Charlie accepted. Had it been Peters here, he'd have pushed. He was good at making enemies.

Back in the car, Charlie shot off a few texts to the uniforms. Where was this backpack and why had it been removed from the crime scene? And by whom? Maybe another look at the scene would help.

Detective Blake parked a block down from Fremont Coffee and suppressed the urge to go inside where creativity happened on the daily. As they walked the quarter mile to the troll, they puzzled over the case. After high school, they'd almost gone to art school and, like Travis, they'd had a few scuffles with the law. But even with their similarities, they couldn't figure why an art student was tagging, let alone tagging the troll.

They stared at the troll's looming shape from across the street. It would've been plenty dark at 3 a.m. They crossed the street and stared at the yellow tape. "What am I missing?" they muttered.

"Are you talking to me, Detective?" asked a nearby officer guarding the crime scene.

They flinched and then laughed when they realized they'd been waiting for the troll to respond and not the officer. Their phone buzzed again. Uniforms had found the vic's backpack in a nearby dumpster. No sketchbook.

When they stepped around the VW Bug, the neon-green tag was present, but now, dark black letters were sprayed over parts of it. "Hey, you got a glove?" they called.

The officer handed them one, and his eyes widened. "That wasn't here an hour ago."

"I know." They touched the paint, and their gloved finger came back black. "Who's been here since the scene was sealed?"

"No one, Detective. Just me."

"And you were here the entire time?"

"Yes, Detective."

They glanced around, but nothing moved. No one approached, and if anyone lurked in the shadows, they remained silent and still. When the detective turned their attention back to the officer, they noted the Fremont Coffee cup in his hand. "When did you get the coffee?"

"Oh! There's a great place just down the street—"

"I know it, but I asked you *when* not *where*."

"Oh, um, about thirty minutes ago. I needed to take a leak and—"

Charlie bit back a string of curse words. "And left the crime scene unattended long enough for the perp to return, right, Officer . . ." They glanced at his badge. "Burke?"

He paled and took a large gulp of coffee. "R-right."

Damn rookie. The troll's hubcap eye followed them as they paced, almost pleading with them to *see* what he'd seen. Beneath the new paint was the half-tag from Travis, but older black paint crept out from around that.

"This wasn't about drugs. This was about art."

This time, when they glanced up at the troll, they could've sworn he was smiling.

ை

I was created out of hate pretending to be art. Yet, I am still art. "Hostile architecture" designed to sweep away the undesirables from under the Aurora Bridge. However, like all created art, once it is born, it no longer belongs to the creator. It escapes. Once out in the world, art belongs to the viewer and whatever the viewer gets out of it, be that a weapon, a tool, a clue, inspiration, history in situ, *or found treasure. Art is what makes the world go round. It can also grind it to a halt.*

In this case, art was the catalyst for the crime and will be the instrument of its justice.

ை

Charlie stifled a yawn behind their binoculars. Their own *Kazza*, whatever it meant, was long dry and the early morning far away as even the bars shut down for the night. Earlier in the day, the idea had come to them. If the crime was about art, then art would bring the perp out of hiding. They'd made a quick stop at the hardware store and one spray can later, they'd left their own mark on the VW Bug. Their bubble letters now covered the perp's tag. A bit crude, but it would get the job done.

The quiet squad car lulled them into a light doze, which they woke from when the binoculars landed in their lap. Of course, Peters couldn't be bothered with a stakeout for a mere "drug deal gone wrong," despite the evidence saying otherwise. Then again, they preferred to work alone.

Something moved beneath a nearby streetlight, and they slouched in their car seat as the figure passed. The scene had been released a few hours earlier, so it wasn't one of theirs out there. Whoever it was didn't head straight for the troll but paused a moment in the shadows before crossing the street. A black hoodie covered the top half of their face, but the detective caught sight of a chiseled chin when they crossed beneath the streetlight. Three minutes passed in the shadows until the figure crossed the street again, this time heading directly for the troll.

They eased out of their squad car, leaving the door leaning against the latch. Sensible sneakers muffled the sound of their steps as they approached. Charlie couldn't see the figure in the dark, but the perp's muttered swears caught their attention.

"What the actual fuck? Are you kidding me?"

Definitely a male. They ducked behind one of the bridge's pillars as they watched him kick the concrete car, then swear as he shook his foot. It was mostly shadows, but their phone picked up his shape and voice well enough as they recorded him.

"You—you know it wasn't my fault, right?" He shook a fist at the troll. "It was an accident. I mean, the little shit messed up my art. This car was *mine*!"

He pulled a spray can from his hoodie pocket and sprayed something over the car. "Dammit!" The perp moved to kick the car again, thought better of it, and then threw the spray paint canister at it instead. "This isn't as good. It'll never be as good. Are you haunting me, you little shit? Damn scholarship kid—should've never been at my school."

Charlie tucked their phone in their pocket, still recording the sounds as they stepped out from behind the pillar. His back was to them as he stared at his art—a jagged black stretch of spirals and lines that could've been anything from tribal to mathematical. As quietly as possible, they pulled their piece from its holster.

"Seattle P.D. Put your hands where I can see them!"

They thought he'd run—most did—but his shoulders slumped as he stared up at the troll a moment before placing his hands above his head.

"You have any weapons or needles on you?"

"No."

Their pat down revealed a wallet with more cash than their monthly paycheck. "William Montgomery, II. What's a boy with all this money doing mixed up in this?"

"Mixed up in what, officer?"

"That's Detective, and before you deny it, I got your little performance on video." They cuffed him and grabbed hold of his hoodie. "We're going to take a little trip to the north precinct where I suspect you've got a lot of explaining to do."

The perp scowled. "The little shit covered up my art. It was the best thing I'd ever done, and he just tagged over it like it was nothing."

"While I admit art is subjective, I'm not sure I would've called those scribbles art."

"You wouldn't understand. Besides, what happened was an accident. I didn't mean to hurt him. Just teach him not to mess with my art. That's not a crime. I'm sure my lawyer can explain that to you, *officer*."

"I'm sure he can also explain the difference between murder and manslaughter to you as well. So what was this art supposed to be anyway?"

"A galaxy."

They glanced over their shoulder toward the troll. While there'd been a bit of poetry to the perp's spirals, nothing about it spoke galaxy to them. A bit creepy how they'd resembled the troll's hubcap eye though.

After tucking Mr. Montgomery into the squad car, they radioed in to the precinct. Maybe after this, they'd stop by and get some coffee. Coffee shops were always open in Seattle.

To be an icon in an iconic city is to always be a target. Never more than a silent witness to a world that moves around me, but always a touchstone in the Emerald City. Even when its streets are wet with rain and other fluids, the City is as beautiful as it is dark. Every once in a while, a light shines, and those that come before me figure it out.

Jennifer Brozek is an award winning author, editor, and tie-in writer. *A Secret Guide to Fighting Elder Gods*, *Never Let Me Sleep*, and *The Last Days of Salton Academy* were finalists for the Bram Stoker Award. She was awarded the Scribe Award for best tie-in Young Adult novel for *BattleTech: The Nellus Academy Incident*. *Grants Pass* won an Australian Shadows Award for best edited publication. A Hugo finalist for Short Form Editor and a finalist for the British Fantasy Award, Jennifer is an active member of SFWA, HWA, and IAMTW. She keeps a tight writing and editing schedule and credits her husband Jeff with being the best sounding board ever. Visit Jennifer's worlds at jenniferbrozek.com or her social media accounts on LinkTree.

Multi-international award-winning speculative fiction author **Raven Oak** (she/they) is best known for *Amaskan's Blood* (2016 Ozma Fantasy Award Winner, Epic Awards Finalist, & Reader's Choice Award Winner), *Amaskan's War* (2018 UK Wishing Award YA Finalist), and *Class-M Exile*. She also has many published short stories in anthologies and magazines. She's even published on the moon! Raven spent most of her K-12 education doodling and writing 500 page monstrosities that are forever locked away in a filing cabinet. Besides being a writer and artist, she's a geeky, disabled ENBY who enjoys getting her game on with tabletop games, indulging in cartography and art, or staring at the ocean. She lives in the Seattle area with her partner, and their three kitties who enjoy lounging across the keyboard when writing deadlines approach. Her hair color changes as often as her bio does, and you can find her at www.ravenoak.net.

The Grandmother Tale
LaShawn M. Wanak

Here, child. Tell me a story.

The only ones I know are from you.

Then tell me one of those.

How about the three witches? That's my favorite one from you.

Hmm. Were they beautiful witches?

Oh yes, Grandmother. They were the most beautiful and deadliest of witches. People would pass by them and fall under their spell without even realizing. No one was immune to their charms: men, women, anyone. The witches were that dangerous.

Describe them to me.

The oldest had skin like pure honey. The birds in the trees often pecked each other to death, so their voices wouldn't compete with hers. She kept her feet warm in a brazier lit from coals of cremated sailors. She also ate chicken hearts like candy.

And the second born?

The second born had eyes white as alabaster, but she bewitched everyone into thinking they were chocolate brown. Visitors would come far and wide to gaze into her wide-set eyes until their bodies turned to stone. She also had a tongue that could whip the stubbornest child bloody and, when she walked, the pavement cracked beneath her heels.

And what about the youngest?

The youngest? Hmm, I'd say she was the most dangerous one of all the three.

Is that so? Why?

Because she was normal.

The third witch lived alone on top of a skyscraper, set in a city jammed with thousands of people. Every morning, she made herself toast and jam and stood in front of the television watching the morning news. Always, always she cried, because she would see so much misery and death taking place. But being the youngest witch, she couldn't do anything about it. You see, she had very little power.

That doesn't make much of a witch.

No, it doesn't. Now, hush—let me tell the story.

The youngest witch couldn't make men beg for one sultry, groin-lengthening gaze. She couldn't make women tremble and clench their thighs from a purred whisper of her lips. She had a plain beauty, a fresh-daisy beauty; one glance and she could easily be forgotten. It didn't bother her all that much. She liked being anonymous.

She worked as a receptionist at a health club down the street from her apartment. She scanned IDs, filed her nails, and scoped out the joggers panting on treadmills. Her boss showed off his new heart tattoo on his perfectly sculpted biceps, and she nodded in appreciation. She bought the same ham-and-swiss rye sandwich for lunch at the corner deli. When her shift was over, she returned to her remote, skyscraper apartment. She watched the news as she dressed all in black—her only testament to her lineage—then, shedding tears, she'd go out to the clubs.

She never paid a cover charge because the bouncers always forgot to charge her. She never danced. Never struck up a conversation. She sat at the darkest corner table with a glass of cream stout, so bitter and so sweet, and ogled the bodies on the dance floor. No one came over to ask her to dance. No one pressed against her or asked if she had plans for the rest of the night.

At promptly nine o'clock, she returned to her apartment, wiped off her makeup, and darned her clothes by the television's fluorescent flicker. When the news stories came on, she would weep and weep and then fall asleep on the couch.

And yet, she treasured her tears. Her softness for the city was an indulgence. Despite the harm the citizens did to each other, the youngest witch savored her own tiny contribution that kept the city running without fail. Thus, the next day, she'd do the same thing. And the next. And the next . . .

All right, I get it. Move to the next part.

Are you sure? I've always liked that part. The witch may not have been interacting with anyone, but she was happy.

Child.

Fine. You're so impatient.

One night, the witch was startled from her sleep by an earth-shattering explosion that shook the apartment around her. She opened her curtains and was shocked to see her city laid waste. Fires raging everywhere. Buildings toppled over. Bodies in the streets. That sort of thing.

What happened?

Some war. It crept up on the city's denizens as they slept. The witch put on her clothes and stepped out into the broken streets. She had only wandered a half block before the building that held her apartment blew up. Survivors streamed around her, screaming, or meandered in the same silent shock as she.

At some point, her foot struck a mangled corpse. She looked down and realized that in her trance-like state, her feet had unconsciously traced the route to her health club. The body was burnt and missing both legs, but she recognized the heart tattoo on her boss's torn bicep.

She realized in that moment that she no longer had a job anymore. Or a home. So, she decided to go to her sisters.

To ask for their help?

Maybe. I don't know. You never really told me why. Perhaps the devastation of the city mirrored the devastation in her heart, and she wanted to tell someone, anyone, to share the burden.

Not likely.

For three days and nights, the witch walked without stopping to eat or drink, indistinguishable from the other glassy-eyed survivors trekking out the city. On the fourth day, she veered from the road and went into the hills alone. She walked until she came to the cave entrance where her sisters dwelled. She went up to the gaping entrance and called their true names, her voice raw from the fires and dust.

After a long time, they shuffled in gauzy robes to stare at the ruined city.

"Not our doing," they said to her.

The youngest sister understood that. There, against the backdrop of the smoke rising from numerous fires, she told them about the city. She talked about the morning hours, the cars clogging the freeways and on-ramps. She told them about the children running to school, the cafés and their fresh warm bagels, the hundreds of thousands of Styrofoam cups containing fresh, fragrant coffee. She told them about the streams of commuters at lunch, the bite of the perfect ham and swiss sandwich on rye. The pounding feet running nowhere on treadmills, and how the musky sweat of those who exercised matched the same sweat rolling down bodies gyrating on a dance floor. She told of bums raising their hands for coins, of cops putting tickets on windshields, of teenagers skateboarding, friends and couples arguing, laughing, breaking up, kissing.

She told of herself, breezing through it all, unseen, untouched, and yet loving it all.

The older sisters listened dutifully, and when the youngest's story finally faltered into exhausted silence, they looked at each other and shrugged.

"Why should we care? There are other cities. Quit bothering us."

Then they went back into their cave, leaving behind only a trace of floral perfume.

Well, that was rude of them.

Was it? When you told me this, you always laughed at this part.

Did I? I guess I did. I always found it hilarious that they turned their backs on her. I take it, though, that she didn't. I can see her now, standing there, fists clenched in fury. What did she do after that?

Something dangerous.

How so?

She went back to the city.

First, she started with the hospitals because that's where most of the survivors congregated. Then, she tackled the sewers. The alleys. Fallout shelters. Basements. She knelt down beside hundreds of pallets and whispered into orphaned ears. She slipped into crowded waiting rooms and orated on top of tables. She cupped her hands around her mouth and shouted from crumbling walls. Her message was the same, no matter who she told.

There are witches living outside the city, and they did nothing to stop its destruction.

Her words spread like a virus: from ear, to mouth, and back to waiting ear. Soon the phrase took on a life of its own as people whispered to one another. A few called for reason—the witches owed the city nothing. Why should they be held responsible?

Then came the lootings. The food shortages. The rape and assaults. The arson.

Rumors began to spread, anger carefully stoked, most of

them stemming from the witches' former lovers. "Witches live outside the city," they complained to the former nail technicians, baristas, and truck drivers, now gathering bricks to heat for warmth, "—witches that hold great power, who could do the unthinkable, the unimaginable. Yet, with all their power, they did nothing to protect the city." They spread their grievances throughout the broken city, refusing to help or clean up, only airing out their resentments, sinking them deep into listening ears. "The witches did nothing! We can't let them get away with that!"

The youngest witch incited it all. She had spent years in the city, watching its citizens, learning its language, drinking its stout. She knew the nasty looks the citizens gave to one another, the rude gestures they made with their fingers. She could hurl insults in so many tongues. She had watched the news every night. She knew what could be borne of ignorance and hate.

For the first time, people began to notice her.

Ah.

The youngest witch no longer dressed in all black, but in pure white. She pulled her hair back into a bun and doffed pince-nez glasses. As the bonfires licked the night sky, she stood on the tallest pile of broken cars, and her shadow leaped with the energy of her impassioned words. Every night she made the crowd chant: "Seize the witches! Make them pay!"

That's my favorite part, you know.

Yes, Grandmother. I know.

A year to the day the city was destroyed, the youngest witch led her new army to her sisters' cave. They weren't taken by surprise. The witches knew what their youngest sister was up to. They weren't witches for nothing. The two sisters hurled their most powerful spells at the torch-wielding mob. Many fell to their deaths, ripping out their hair, their clothes, their tongues. Others collapsed and humped the dirt, crying out in pained ecstasy. But the youngest witch had taught the people well. They stepped over the fallen and threw themselves forward and, as they fell, others took their place.

For many nights, they fought like this, but even witches tire. It wasn't long before their arms trembled, and their voices grew weak. The youngest witch urged the remainder of her army forward. They overpowered the two witches, grabbed them by their hair, clapped blindfolds over their eyes, wrapped iron chains around their bodies. They dragged the witches back to the city, chained them to the remains of what used to be City Hall.

There, they did so many unspeakable things. I can't even relate them to you. I can only say the youngest witch watched it all, impassive. The only movement she displayed was the reflection of the bonfires in her eyeglasses.

When the mob finished, she approached her sisters, gestured to the guards to force their heads up. She leaned down to peer into their ravaged faces.

"Just because I don't have power," she hissed. "Doesn't mean I can't use it."

She gave the signal to the mob to kill them.

What a gruesome way to die.

Yes, it certainly is.

I would never want to die like that. Promise me I won't die like that.

I promise. Shall I finish the story?

When the deed was over, the youngest witch—the only witch now—turned to thank the mob, ready to instruct them into the hard task of rebuilding the city. Instead, she met hardened gazes, the striking of steel pipes on concrete, the smack of wooden bats against fleshy palms. Desperate, she searched for someone, anyone, who would speak up in her defense, but no one did. The blood of her sisters still ran warm under her feet. "What are you doing? I'm the one who leads you! If it wasn't for me, you'd be lost, cowering by your fires, turning on each other like starving, desperate rats. You can't do this!"

But they could. And they did. Do you know why, Grandmother?

. . .

… *because it doesn't matter if you have powers or not. In the end, a witch is a witch is a witch.*

So, there is no need, really, for me to tell you what they did to her.

And without her sisters, there was no one she could turn to for help.

They tortured her. They gouged out her eyes. Sliced into her flesh. Hours and days without end.

Until she could barely think, poor thing.

And then, they did the most brutal thing of all. What did they do, Grandmother?

They kept her alive. They didn't let her die. They chained her inside the lowest, darkest room they could find. They hooked her to machines that pumped blood, made her breathe. They forced her to tell this story over and over and over again. And whenever she tried to change even one word, they took another piece from her. Her feet, her arms, her legs, hands. Organs.

But they left her heart, so she could still feel.

Ah. Yes. So that I would never forget.

And to care for you, they sought among themselves those who had the tendency to become witches. Loners, dreamers, debaters, mutes. Unaware of their witchy powers, they were uprooted from their lives and forced to become your caretakers. They corralled us into this place, forced us to feed you, care for you.

Call you 'Grandmother.'

Because the worst thing you can do to a witch is force them to love someone other than themselves.

I'm sorry, Grandmother. This was not the end I promised you. You must be so tired.

I am. Will they bring another group after you leave?

I don't think you'll need to worry about that. Here, let me get your pillow.

. . .

. . .

There. Rest now. You've had enough.

I don't have much time; once things start to collapse, they'll come here to check on you. When they see that you're gone, they'll find another witch to blame.

But we won't let them, my sisters and I.

Witches and cities are more alike than you think, Grandmother. Both can be callous, selfish, cruel. And yet, your stories contained such beauty, you can't help but love them. You taught us that, Grandmother. It's why we love you.

Unlike you and your sisters, however, we're stronger when we work together.

We're going to tell the city a new story. One that doesn't involve callous witches or murderous mobs. With our power, we'll find a way to bring back the city you once loved. And maybe, if our power is strong enough, we'll find a way to make the city love you back.

So, while we're waiting: here, Grandmother, let me tell you a story.

LaShawn M. Wanak writes speculative stories, essays, and poetry. Her work is published in venues such as *Uncanny Magazine* and *FIYAH*. She served as the lead writer for the art collective Meow Wolf on their permanent immersive exhibit, *The Real Unreal*, in Grapevine, TX. She is also the editor of the Hugo-nominated online magazine *GigaNotoSaurus*. LaShawn enjoys knitting, anime, and wrestling with theological truths from a Womanist's perspective. You can find her on Facebook, Bluesky, her website *The Cafe in the Woods*, and her Substack newsletter. She also has a Patreon.

Writing stories keeps her sane. Also, pie.

For a Thousand Silver Blessings
Bryan Young

Glasha awoke to the sound of a harsh whisper, a habit leftover from the rough days of a life she left behind. That her name was the word that woke her caused old panic to stir. When she realized where and *when* she was, she felt safer, but not by much. She'd need to know what was going on to feel safe enough to drift back to sleep in the privacy of her covered wagon.

". . . it's a reward," came the sound of whispering.

She recognized the voice. Loren. Normally kind. It was his troupe she joined when she gave up her previous life.

Given the speaker, she hoped she was safe enough to return to her slumber, but she didn't like the tremored edge of temptation in his voice.

Gripping the hilt of the sword she kept between her straw mattress and the wooden frame of the wagon—a sword they didn't know she'd kept—she braced for trouble. The real sword always felt more comfortable in her hands than the stage weapons they entertained folks with. Holding it made her feel solid and real. She was never more alive than when she could fend off death with a blade.

It helped that she was good at it, too.

Maybe the best.

"Yeah," the other voice whispered. "A thousand silver blessings."

"For her?" Loren sounded incredulous. The voices came from the other side of the waxed canvas cover.

Her wagon usually brought up the rear of the acting troupe's caravan, so they weren't just idly hanging by. They were there for no good.

"Look at the poster," the second voice said. Glasha recognized it as Janith's. Janith was the troupe's leading lady and though she never talked about her past—not any more than Glasha talked of hers—Glasha got the distinct impression her history was every bit as checkered. Where Glasha wanted to forget, it seemed like Janith was coming back to her roots. "It's her. Plain as day. Right down to the filed-down orc tusks."

Glasha suppressed a sigh, and disappointment blossomed in her middle. She'd finally felt like she'd found a home not predicated on her ability to shed the blood of others. The life of an orc in the human world was difficult enough as it was, but there was this pervasive view that all they were good at was violence.

Glasha never wanted to play that game again if she could help it, but if Loren and Janith really wanted to, she was going to make sure she held all the cards and made the ante a price too dear for them to pay.

"It *is* her," Loren admitted. "But do we really do this? She's been good to us."

As they debated, Glasha sought out the best way to slip from the wagon without being noticed. Most likely, their plan would be to catch her while they thought she was sleeping. If they were coming for her, she'd do well to get to them first. She still didn't want to hurt them, though, even if they were aiming daggers at her.

They'd been good to her and taken her in when she needed it, and that wasn't something she'd easily forget, even if they saw silver blessings glistening in their eyes like twinkling fairy lights.

"Loren, think about it. A thousand silver blessings would carry us for years. Hell, five would keep the whole troupe fed for a month. Can we afford *not* to turn her in?"

"I suppose not," Loren said.

Their intentions made the decision for her. The best way to escape was down. There had been a trap door in the wagon's floor leading to the ground below. She'd practiced many nights opening it without a sound, just as a precaution. She'd oiled the hinge often and kept it well operating, and hidden with a rug over the seams. Just in case strangers came in snooping. It had been one of the old troupe wagons, and she'd been lent its use, but the way the hinges had rusted over told her she was probably the only one who realized it was there.

Peeling back the carpet and lifting the door, Glasha found she could still move silently if she wanted. Not all the old skills had left her. Some of the things she'd learned would remain etched into her instincts like carvings on a rock, markers for generations beyond.

Though she couldn't put the rug back, she could gently ease the trap door back into place from below without a sound.

Gripping the sword and descending quietly to the ground beneath the wagon, Glasha surveyed her situation. Their feet pointed at each other on the other side of the rear wagon wheel, still debating in loud whispers about their intended course of action.

Had she been a heavier sleeper, they'd have been able to get the drop on her.

In the past, Glasha would have simply come out swinging. Old Glasha was angry and sad, and her blood was up. But the new Glasha, the compassionate Glasha, Glasha the traveling Bard, had more scruples than that. Her choice ahead was difficult.

"It says dead or alive," Loren whispered. "You think she'd give herself up alive and split some of the reward? We'd cut her in . . ."

No, Glasha thought. If she gave herself up, they'd get her hung or burned before she could see a hint of one of those silver blessings.

No way would she agree to give herself up. Especially since the people looking for her probably weren't the law, she hadn't crossed king or crown to get into trouble. It was the Bounty Hunter's Guild, which was even worse. And if they'd gotten a poster into Janith's hands, that meant bounty hunters would be snooping around.

"Would you give yourself up if you didn't have to?" Janith asked him.

When he offered no response, Glasha filled in the rest, imagining him shaking his head sadly. Exactly like she would if she were being asked that same question.

When the talking stopped altogether and their feet meandered to the back of the wagon, she started to worry about making her choice.

Their shins were there, bare and ready to strike. Even crouched beneath the wagon, she could slash bloody all four legs she saw, shredding them enough to keep them from running after her.

Unfortunately, she was committed to doing them a kindness, unless they forced her to do otherwise.

So she slowly pushed herself back toward the front of the wagon as they silently made their way toward the rear entrance. They would discover she was missing a in a matter of moments, and her move had to be made now, imperfect as it may have been.

Crouched low beneath the wagon, Glasha considered bolting forward, cresting the protection of the wagon and racing to the thicket beyond the meadow. Around her back were the tight straps of her emergency bag, for just such a situation. She'd vowed a long time ago to never be caught unprepared, and her instincts had served her well. Out there on her own she'd be able to survive for a while. A quiet voice inside her told her to stay, though. This was home and she wanted to resolve things peacefully if she could.

Watching their feet, she saw Loren and Janith creep softly into the back of her wagon, the dark of night obscuring the vestiges of the camp beyond. The communal fire had died out in the earlier, small hours of the morning, so only the moon could tell the secrets of their dark business.

Another moment passed. Would they make a commotion when they discovered her missing? She considered fleeing then, but if there were bounty hunters nearby, she knew they would just pick up her trail and give deadly chase.

Besides, she had nowhere to go and no one to turn to.

Glasha had learned a long time ago that you had to do plenty of things you didn't like in order to survive. Some worse than others. Some more distasteful, some more questionable. But in the end, she'd always made it through, and she had no intention of losing this time.

The decision to stay felt prescient when Janith's signature scream shattered the night. Sometimes, that scream was what folks would come from miles away to hear. And to see what situation she was put in to elicit such a shriek. It was a blood-curdling screech, perfect to raise the hairs on the end of every arm and back of every neck in an audience. But now, that piercing keen didn't bode well for Glasha.

It meant her former family intended to find her and fight.

They would not wait until morning to fly into action.

She glanced at the rest of the camp from her prone position, torches lit up around the caravan, and a commotion ensued. Loren and Janith made their way to the front and held court. She knew they would spend time explaining themselves, but what would they tell the other actors and hands in the troupe? That they'd decided to turn on one of their own? That there were a thousand silver blessings in it for them if they betrayed the she-orc?

Likely.

Glasha decided to deal with that emotional weight later. She had to worry about surviving in the near term. She still didn't want to hurt anyone.

When she heard the gallop of horses heading in all directions to search for her, she knew she had to make her move quickly and while they were gone.

Clearing the wagon and rising quietly to her bare feet, Glasha looked around the camp, emptied of most of the troupe. No doubt they were chasing her for the blessings. Creeping around on tiptoes in the silver moonlight, Glasha knew Loren wouldn't go do the dirty work himself, and she had to speak with him if she was going to keep more blood from staining her hands.

Unfortunately, the figure standing watch with a torch between her and Loren's carriage was going to be a problem. Squinting, she decided it looked like Duerte, the troupe's leading man. He spent as much time playing the heavy as the hero. For a human, he was handsome and well-built but, up until recently, Glasha had saved her fawning eyes for Janith.

Her stomach soured, thinking about that particular mistake. Putting her daydreams of Janith out of her mind, she set it to the task of Duerte.

She was going to have to go through him to get to Loren.

Her only advantage against Duerte was the knowledge that all his swordplay training was for the stage. He flourished his blade with the audience in mind, not survival.

Glasha padded softly across the grass, staying in the shadows of his torch.

How could he have known to stay behind? Had he been ordered to keep watch? Did he just have more luck than brains? That was how Glasha's grandmother would have put it.

The gnarled voice of Glasha's grandmother echoed in her head. "More luck than brains, that one, don't tangle with those, they'll beat you at your own game, sure as anything. Probably sitting on horseshoes."

Duerte must have been sleeping in his costume from that day's performance because he was still dressed like a foppish noble.

Relying on the old instincts, Glasha waited, anticipating his moves, stepping only when his attention was directed elsewhere. He didn't have the wherewithal or the experience to realize he was prey.

He scanned the ground from one side of the encampment to the other, never once thinking to look right behind him.

Like a jungle cat, Glasha pounced Duerte. The pair tumbled to the ground, the torch flew and fell into the tall grass out of their reach, and Glasha hoped she could deal with Duerte and get to the flame before she set the entire forest ablaze and the camp with it. It was decidedly more difficult to escape through fire than forest.

Duerte muscled back at her, struggling to get his hands purchased somewhere on her body, but Glasha planned the angle of her tackle carefully, timing and controlling it so she ended up astride him, her bulky green hands pinning him to the ground at the shoulders.

He pawed at her, but she shifted her grip from shoulders to wrists, leaving him to struggle, defenseless.

Duerte took a breath to scream, but when he made eye contact with Glasha, she let out a low growl from the top of her chest that rumbled through the gravel of her throat.

Terror filled Duerte's eyes like tears, and he closed his mouth with a frightened gulp.

"I don't want to kill you, Duerte," Glasha said, in a low whisper. "But don't think I won't if I don't have to."

"I, uhh . . . ," he said.

He squirmed, but somehow he found his courage.

"She's—!" he screamed, just as she thought he might play nice. Glasha suppressed a roar and covered his mouth with her meaty palm and growled deeply at him.

Widening her eyes and baring her teeth, she assumed he'd never seen such terror before. His mouth turned from defiant grin to terrified frown. His eyebrows turned up in fright.

Below her, she felt a warm moisture spread.

Confused, she looked down at his middle. Then her confusion was replaced by disgust. "Did you just piss yourself?"

Instead of answering, Duerte quietly sobbed.

Some actor he was.

"Listen," she told him. "I'm going to have a little chat with Loren, and then leave here. You can't possibly stop me. None of you can. You'll never see me again."

He made no reply, his mouth still held shut. He just cringed when her breath landed hot on his face.

"Just let me leave in peace."

Glasha knew if he kept up all that noise, he'd alert Loren and anyone else still in the caravan to her presence . . . if he hadn't already.

So she did what she had to. She hit him across the head, making sure to aim the side of her fist right against his temple. And suddenly, the silence returned and Duerte went limp.

Silent and still, in the growing gray light of morning and with no blood on her hands, she approached the lead carriage. Loren's. The fanciest of them all, decorated in red paint with golden flourishes of hand-carved gingerbread. Across the side, printed in matching golden lettering, were the words: "Blackfriar's Playing Company." Below that, the subtitle offered promises of entertainment and light adventuring to those who could pay.

No one ever took them up on the adventuring, but every town they visited wanted a play.

It was the only wagon with a lit lantern glowing orange at the seams from inside that cut into the softness of dawn.

There she would go. To end it.

Approaching cautious and quiet, she made her way through the other carriages, ensuring that no one else had been left on guard. There was no sense in alerting them to her presence. When she reached Loren's wagon, she put her ear to it and listened. She heard vague movements. Someone was definitely inside.

As Glasha came across the front of the carriage, the horse bridled to it whinnied.

Stepping up onto the buckboard, Glasha opened the door that led from the bench at the front to the wagon's interior. It was appointed lushly; of course it had to be because they had a reputation to maintain. The walls were strewn with fancy silks and laced curtains. Everything was upholstered in silk for when they entertained nobles or did their scrying act with crystal balls and minor magic.

Sitting there, at the small desk to one side, was Loren.

His back was to Glasha.

"Why did you take me in if you were just going to turn on me?" she asked.

Startled, he turned to see her hunched over inside his

sanctum. She closed the door behind her, never loosening her grip on her sword's hilt.

Loren sighed. His face was tired, his posture deflated. "I didn't want to."

"All you had to do was let me go."

She watched him closely, watching the muscles in his arms tense and relax in turn beneath his cotton shirt. She could read the body language of fighters, but bards had always been more difficult. They'd been much better trained to obscure the language their bodies spoke. But still, even with Loren's mastery of his trade, she couldn't help but feel that he coiled like a snake, ready to strike. Her eyes traveled along his form, wondering where he might have a weapon hidden.

Was that smug half-grin on his face the sign of an edge?

"I wanted to let you go. Trust me. I've had no problem with you, Glash. Hells of fire, I even *like* you. A lot. I thought you were going to be trouble when you came to us and we took you in, but you've been a downright asset."

"But not a thousand blessings worth?"

Loren laughed. A true, deep laugh. "*I'm* not even worth that much. If Janith came in here with a wanted poster from the guild offering a thousand blessings for me, I'd expect her to take it."

Glasha kept scanning the room, drinking in the sight, hoping to find whatever it was Loren was obscuring. There was a trunk behind where Loren sat. Large enough to fit Janith. Usually, it was filled with costumes and props, but she could have easily packed it down and fit inside with her slight frame. Glasha moved to it, shoulders hunched to keep her head from ramming into the ceiling, and sat firmly on the costume trunk. If Janith—or anyone else—was hiding in there, she wasn't going to make it easy for them to ambush her.

Loren spun around to keep his eyes on Glasha and that's when she noticed the hilt of the dagger beneath his shirt.

Seeing it, she flashed her blade in his direction. No doubt he thought she had no room to swing it, but you didn't need to swing a sword to stick a pig. "You just keep your hands on the desk and sit there nice and easy. I don't want any trouble."

"You gonna kill me?"

She really didn't want to, but couldn't bring herself to say it. "It's not like you're gonna just let me walk out of here otherwise. Are you?"

"What if I did?"

Glasha had convinced herself she was going to have to kill him, but his offer was enough to give her pause.

She could start over again.

She hadn't wanted to kill anyone ever again. That was why she joined Blackfriar's in the first place.

"Fine then," she said. "You let me go, and no one follows. If the bounty hunters and wage rangers come looking for me, you point 'em in the wrong direction. That's easy enough and worth your hide, yes?"

"Sounds fair to me."

Glasha lowered her sword, taking the point from his back. "Deal. Now put your dagger up on the table and keep your hands away from it," she told him.

"How did you know?"

"There's a lot about me you don't know, Loren."

He placed the dagger on the table as she asked and raised his hands in mock surrender. "I guess that explains the bounty."

"Keep your hands there," she said, heading to the larger door at the rear of the wagon and the freedom beyond.

As soon as her weight came off the trunk, it flung open.

In a flash, Loren reached for the dagger, and Janith emerged from the trunk, wielding a crossbow and facing the wrong direction.

Loren threw his dagger at Glasha.

Raising her sword, fast as lightning, she hoped to parry the knife.

She missed, but his aim had been off. The tip dragged across her bicep rather than piercing her heart.

Blood seeped down her arm, each drop a rivulet of pain she chose to ignore.

Janith spun in place, doing her best to get a shot with the crossbow, but by then Glasha ran on survival instinct and stuck that proverbial pig without a swing. The blade pierced Janith's chest and turned her pretty silk dress red with blood.

With a roar, Loren lunged for Glasha.

She swatted him from the air with a backhand as though she were shooing a fly. Her hand connected with his soft cheek, and she felt a tooth break loose on impact. Loren hit the side of the wagon with a dull thud and collapsed into the trunk atop Janith's prostrate form.

Torn and bleeding, she debated just leaving him there for the others to find, but he rose of his own volition. This time, he fumbled with the crossbow himself, having taken it from Janith's dead hands.

"Damn it, Glasha," he said, baring his bloodied teeth.

Before he could fire, Glasha entangled the tip of her sword through the crossbow and placed it against Loren's chest.

He triggered the release, but the bolt never flew.

His eyes widened, and his curtain called.

Glasha played her ace. Lunging deeper with the sword, she dragged the tip upward, tearing through his body.

Brutal but efficient.

And she hated herself for it.

They were good people.

She paused. Breathing heavily. Watching all the blood flow from the two new corpses she'd made.

And for what?

"Damn you," she said as though they could hear. "Damn you both."

But if there was anything Glasha was good at, it was surviving.

And survive she would.

She collected what she could from Loren's opulent wagon, fattened her bag, and lit off into the rising heat of the blue morning.

Heading out toward the trees where the fewest tracks led, she hoped for a fresh start.

That's all she wanted.

But if trouble sought her out, she'd be ready for it.

She always was.

On soft, bare feet she left the camp. At the edge of the trees on the far side of the meadow, she turned back to see the encampment of wagons she'd called home for the better part of a year.

She sighed.

One day . . .

One day she might have a peace more than fleeting.

Turning back around, Glasha set out into the woods, seeking blessings of her own. Not silver or gold. Not even platinum. But those that couldn't be bought or sold. Blessings of peace and plenty.

That was all she wanted.

And that was all she'd hoped for anyone else.

Bryan Young (he/they) works across many different media. His work as a writer and producer has been called "filmmaking gold" by *The New York Times*. He's also published comic books with Slave Labor Graphics and Image Comics. He's been a regular contributor for the *Huffington Post*, StarWars.com, *Star Wars Insider* magazine, SYFY, /Film, and was the founder and editor in chief of the geek news and review site Big Shiny Robot! In 2014, he wrote the critically acclaimed history book, *A Children's Illustrated History of Presidential Assassination*. He co-authored *Robotech: The Macross Saga* RPG and has written five books in the BattleTech Universe: *Honor's Gauntlet, A Question of Survival, Fox Tales, Without Question*, and the forthcoming *VoidBreaker*. His latest nonfiction tie-in book, *The Big Bang Theory Book of Lists* is a #1 Bestseller on Amazon. His work has won two Diamond Quill awards and in 2023 he was named Writer of the Year by the League of Utah Writers. He teaches writing for *Writer's Digest, Script Magazine,* and at the University of Utah. Follow him across social media @swankmotron or visit swankmotron.com.

Kicking Santa's Ass
Richard Dansky

Tonight was the night Jimmy Connolly was going to kick Santa Claus's ass.

He took a pull on his Yvengling longneck and rocked back and forth on his porch. It was a typical December night in south Philly: just a hint of snow on the ground and more than a hint of dirt on that snow. It was cold, maybe mid-twenties, but he didn't care. The beer was keeping him warm. That, and his righteous indignation.

He'd hired a Santa Claus, you see. Hired one for his son Patrick's Christmas party. All the kid wanted was to see Santa and feed him some homemade cookies, so Jimmy dug deep into the money he'd been saving and called an agency, one of those places that rented out clowns and people in funny costumes to parties and store openings and what have you. Do you have Santa Claus, he'd asked, and he'd been told yes. And then he'd arranged for Santa to stop by Patrick's party.

But that was the funny thing. The party came and went, and no Santa. Sure, Patrick had a good time, but the kid really wanted Santa, and he'd been promised Santa. And Santa was a no-show, just like Jimmy's miserable drunk of a brother-in-law. So, after the party was over, Jimmy got on the horn with the party people.

And they had lied to him, he was sure of it. No way he would have booked Santa for the wrong date. There was no way he'd get that date wrong. Patrick had been so looking forward to it, and those sons of bitches insisted that he'd scheduled Santa for tonight, not last night. They said they had a contract and everything.

Well, if Santa was coming tonight, Jimmy thought, Santa was gonna learn what it means to disappoint Jimmy Connolly's little boy.

He stood up and finished the beer, then reached down to the case at his feet for another one. He popped the lid, then took a long swig. From inside the house, he could hear the sound of the Eagles game. They were losing to Minnesota. It figured.

"Jimmy?" That was his wife, Heather. She stepped out onto the porch, a cigarette in one hand and all bundled up in a winter coat. "Jesus, Jimmy, you're gonna catch your death out here."

And she had a point. All Jimmy was wearing was a pair of jeans with shitkicker boots and a sleeveless T-shirt he'd picked up playing carny games down the Shore. It said "OCEAN CITY" in faded blue letters on the front, a relic of summers gone.

"Cold doesn't bother me none, babe. I'm just waiting for Santa Claus."

She took a quick puff on her cigarette and shook her head. "That makes me so mad, them disappointing a little kid like that. That Santa Claus shows up, you give him a piece of your mind, you hear me?"

"I hear you, babe."

"And you don't pay him nothing. We hired him for the party, and he didn't show, so he gets nothing." She took another drag on the cigarette—she tried to avoid smoking inside the house, 'cause the doctor had said it was bad for Patrick—then stubbed the butt out on the porch. "Goddamn it's cold. It's too cold to smoke, even. You should really put on a jacket, hon."

"I'm plenty warm, babe. Trust me. And that Santa's gonna get everything that's coming to him."

Her eyes held his for a minute. "Don't be getting yourself in trouble, James Michael Connolly. I don't need the police coming by because you got too excited."

"I won't get excited, I swear," he said, slipping his off hand behind his back to cross his fingers. "I'm just mad for Patrick— that's all. It'll be a clean, elegant discussion." He smiled, and then he belched.

"All right, Jimmy. I trust you. Love you." She blew him a kiss with nicotine-stained fingers and clambered back into the house. He watched her go, then started pacing up and down on the porch. It was past 6, and the city was already covered in darkness. The streetlamps buzzed as they cast their yellowish light down on the sidewalks and asphalt. Cars rolled by, splattering half-melted slush everywhere, and Jimmy waited. His beer joined the empties, and then another one did, and then another. Inside, the Eagles were dying by slow strangulation.

And still, Jimmy waited.

The party last night had been set for 6:30. If Santa was a timely son of a bitch, and he'd kind of have to be, delivering all those presents—the thought gave Jimmy a chuckle—then he'd be here any minute, and the ass beating could commence.

Finally, at 6:27, a beat-up Chevy Impala drove past the

house, slowly, flashers on. The driver was either lost or looking for a parking spot, and Jimmy knew which way he was betting. The car pulled over about three houses down and proceeded to embark on a painfully awkward bout of parallel parking. It must have taken the driver six or seven back-and-forths to get into the space, with a bumper tap on either end for good measure.

Jimmy was off the porch before the door of the car opened, and the Santa Claus stepped out. The guy waved, then leaned back into the car to emerge with a red bag with white trim. "Ho ho ho," the Santa said, but there was something wrong.

A few more steps and he had it—Santa was just too damn small. This wasn't a fat man with a beard, or even a man in a fat suit. It was a kid—a teenager with a pillow under his belt and a fake beard that was dangling precariously off one ear. Sure, he was wearing a Santa suit, red velour with white fur trim and black boots along with a Santa hat, but he wasn't Santa.

Not even close.

The thought filled him with sudden rage. He'd wanted to kick Santa's ass before for not showing. Now he was imagining the look on Patrick's face when this fucking kid walked through the door. It would have been a goddamned riot.

And now Santa Kid was walking across the street toward him, bag of candy canes slung over his shoulder. "Mister Connolly? Hi, I'm—"

Jimmy didn't let him finish. He just popped him one, right in the nose, and Santa went down like he'd been shot. "Owww!" he said, and put his gloved hands to his face as he lay in the street. The bag of candy canes sat a few feet away, forgotten.

"Get up," Jimmy said. "I'm not going to kick you while you're down, but you've got it coming to you for disappointing my kid."

"What are you talking about?" the Santa asked frantically, and Jimmy realized how young he really was. Sixteen, maybe seventeen, tops—but that didn't excuse him for standing up Patrick. Or for not being any kind of real Santa. The kid scrambled to his knees and started crawling back toward the Impala.

Good enough, Jimmy decided, and kicked him in the ribs. Santa collapsed onto the wet street and moaned. "What are you doing, mister? I'm just a party Santa."

"You were supposed to be here yesterday," Jimmy said, relentless. "My son wanted Santa at his Christmas party. Instead, he got nothing, and instead of nothing, he would have gotten *you.*" He accented the last line with another kick, and Santa rolled over on his back. His nose was bleeding, the red spreading into the cheap, cockeyed beard.

"Please, mister," the kid pleaded. "You don't want to do this. And the costume? It's a rental. If I bring it back all messed up, I'm going to get in so much trouble."

"You don't understand, do you?" Jimmy said. "You're already in trouble. Now get up, so I can knock you on your ass again."

In response, the kid scrambled to his feet and ran. Jimmy gave a whoop and a holler and pelted off after him. Santa got to the Impala and went around the other side to put the mass of the vehicle between himself and his pursuer. Clearly, his plan was to get into the car and get away, but Jimmy was having none of it. He slammed into the fender to slow his momentum, and began pursuing the kid around the car.

As soon as he saw Jimmy coming around the front of the big sedan, the kid went the other way toward the back. They went around and around, the kid hoping to buy a big enough lead that he could pop open the door and get inside, Jimmy staying hot on his heels.

And then, inevitably, it happened. The kid in the Santa suit hit some ice as he was digging around the hood and ate it right on the sidewalk. Jimmy was on him in a flash, grabbing him by the scruff of the neck and pulling him up. "Nothing personal, kid," he said. "But someone's got to pay."

The kid tried to wriggle loose and got nowhere. "Please," he said. "You so don't want to do this. Just let me go. You can keep the candy canes. Just let me go."

"On no, I'm not done with you yet." Jimmy raised his arm for a swing, and so help him God, the kid *snarled*.

Startled, Jimmy dropped his hand down and stared. It looked like the kid was having some kind of seizure, and for the first time, Jimmy worried he might get in trouble for this, that he might have gone just a little too far.

Then the kid got up. Only it wasn't the kid anymore. What rose up from the ground was a *thing*, still rippling and shifting from human form into something huge and furred, with a fanged snout and predator's eyes. "I told you," it said, "to let me go. Now look what you've made me do." The beast gestured dramatically at its outfit, "Ruined. And like you said, somebody's got to pay." One clawed hand reached out and rested heavily on Jimmy's shoulder. "Thank God you were my last stop tonight."

Jimmy's eyes bulged. What he was seeing he couldn't believe.

The Yvenglings swirled heavy and unpleasant in his gut and, distantly, he realized the ass-kicking might be going the other way after all. "Easy there," he heard himself saying. "I'm sure we can talk this out."

"Oh no." The creature—Jimmy was pretty sure it was a werewolf at this point, but he didn't want to ask—gave him a gentle shove, and Jimmy stumbled backward. "You had your chance. You decided to be a dick. Well, two can play at that game." It took a graceful step forward, feet exploding out of the Santa boots in every direction. "You want to know a secret? Changing really takes it out of you. You do it, and you get so God-awful hungry it's barely worth it half the time." He jabbed Jimmy in the shoulder, and Jimmy could feel the sharp claw on his bare skin. "You know what you look like to me right now? You look like a frightened rabbit. And you know what rabbits do?" The beast leaned in conspiratorially.

"What?" said Jimmy. He licked his lips. They were dry, and his throat was tight.

"They run." The werewolf gave Jimmy a shove that spun him around and half-knocked him down. "Run, little rabbit. Run!"

Jimmy ran. The beast ran after him, steam rising from its nostrils in the cold night air.

Not daring to look over his shoulder, Jimmy cut across the street and headed back toward his house. If he could just get inside, he could bolt the door, and then he'd be safe. Maybe.

Then again, maybe not. And if that thing got inside, where Heather and Patrick were—no, better to just keep running and lead it as far away as possible from his family.

His feet slapped wet on the sidewalk as he ran, while the creature loped after him silently. Where to go, where to go? A thought came to Jimmy—he could slip into the backyard and over the fence, and get away that way. He imagined hot breath on the back of his neck—or was he imagining it? Was the monster that close?—and swerved up Old Man Przewski's driveway.

Away from the streetlights, it got dark in a hurry. Jimmy fumbled with the latch on the gate to the backyard, every second imagining those claws ripping into him. He got the gate open and slipped through. Then he slammed it in the face of the onrushing werewolf.

Who promptly vaulted the gate with dangerous ease, landing in the backyard among the old man's lawn furniture. There was a crash and a clatter, and a pair of chairs went down, and then the werewolf was off and moving again.

Jimmy had already scaled a fence and was running through the next backyard. The werewolf thundered after him, and even as he hopped another fence, Jimmy realized that he was being herded back to his house. But how did the monster know?

Of course. The address for the party. The damn thing knew exactly where he was going. And then it was up and over another fence and down and then he was stumbling over Patrick's sandbox and sprawling in the wet sand and dirt.

The beast landed next to him with a thud and a grunt a moment later. "No more running," it said, and put one weighty foot on Jimmy's back to make sure he couldn't move.

For the first time, Jimmy began seriously considering the fact that he might not make it out of this alive. He began praying under his breath, *Oh God, don't let Patrick see this*. He was suddenly sure the end was coming soon, and it was going to be messy, and he didn't want his son to witness it.

And then, as if God were laughing at him, a window opened. Second floor, in the back of the house. Patrick's room. And there was that familiar small shape silhouetted in the window. "Daddy? Is that you, Daddy? Are you and Santa fighting?"

Jimmy opened his mouth to say something, anything to reassure his kid when, to his surprise, the werewolf spoke up. "No, Patrick. Your Daddy and I are just playing. He'll be in in a moment." He leaned down and growled. "Won't you?"

"Err, yes! Yes, that's it!" Jimmy called, desperate with relief. Then, lower, "You're going to let me go?"

"I'm not going to eat a kid's dad in front of him on Christmas, no," said the werewolf. "Though believe me—I was tempted. Now I'm going to let you up, and then we're going to settle up, and you're going to remember this the next time you think about picking on someone smaller than yourself."

"I'll remember. I swear."

"Good." The foot lifted off his back. "The way I see it, you owe me fifty bucks for the party. Plus, we'll be billing you for the Santa costume."

"Waitaminute. The party was yesterday!"

"Not my fault you scheduled for the wrong date. I showed up, didn't I?" The werewolf grinned, showing all of his teeth. There were a great many of them, and they all looked sharp. "So I'm going to let get off the ground, and you're going to pony up, and then that will be that. Unless you've got a better idea."

"No . . . no . . . " Jimmy clambered to his feet, his front caked with dirt and sand. "Hang on, let me get my wallet." He dug into his jeans and pulled it out, then opened it up and yanked out a couple of twenties and a ten. "But I'm not tipping you."

"I'm not surprised," said the monster, and then suddenly it was just the kid again in a raggedy Santa suit. "Really, you've got to check your dates."

"Yeah, well." Jimmy had nothing to say to that. Then he surprised himself. "Err, you want to come in for some hot chocolate or a cup of coffee or something?"

"I think that would be a very bad idea," said the kid, "but thank you. Like I said, keep the bag with the candy canes, if they haven't all melted by now." And then he turned and walked off.

Jimmy just stood there and watched him go, until Heather turned on the back lights and came out on the porch to yell at him.

A twenty-five-year veteran of the video game industry, **Richard Dansky** is an internationally respected expert in the field of game narrative, with credits on franchises like *Hunt: Showdown*, *The Division*, *Splinter Cell*, *Might and Magic*, and many more. He has published eight novels and two short story collections, most recently *A Meeting In The Devil's House*. Richard was also a major contributor to White Wolf's legendary *World of Darkness* tabletop RPG setting, and for a brief moment, he was the world's leading expert on Denebian Slime Devils.

The Goblin's Locket

Gregory A. Wilson

"Perhaps," Lock observed with the slightest smile, "it will be easier if you simply paint them all the same."

The goblin to which he addressed this comment, sitting at a table in the living room of the apartment the two friends shared, looked up slowly. Despite the size of the magnifying goggles Wat was wearing, which made him look vaguely like a large insect, Lock could still see the sour expression on his face. "Easier, as you should know, isn't better. And if some of the human commanders of the Cannisian Royals think all goblins look the same, I don't."

"As a goblin, obviously I don't either," Lock said, his smile widening. "I thought you all had the same uniform, though."

Wat snorted. "Spoken like a civvy." He pointed the paintbrush he was holding at one of the miniature figures on the table in front of him, a soldier in armor, wielding sword and shield. "This here's a Regular, from the rank and file of the Third Goblin Division. See the detail on that shield? Standard issue. Wouldn't catch an officer with one of these. Now this one—" He waved his brush at another, slightly larger figure to the right. "This is an officer. Different sword, different epaulets, red and gold accents. I can't paint both of these the same way." His face twisted as if appalled by the concept.

"Fair enough," Lock said, shrugging as he returned to his chair where he had been reading the latest issue of the *Cannis Gazette*. "But you've been at that now for days, and judging from your reactions every few minutes, it hasn't been the . . . smoothest process." He picked up the discarded paper from the chair and sat as the burly goblin at the table scowled. "How many figures do you need for this?" he asked after a moment.

"Fifty's a small number, not even half as many as the Third usually has, but it's as many as I'll be able to get done in time for the reunion," Wat said. "It's Emson's fault; I can't figure why he waited until the week before to tell me about it. Not like anyone else from that division has a lick of sense, but he's the commander . . . it was up to him to arrange it."

Lock looked up from his paper to see Wat carefully dipping his latest paintbrush in the small well of silver paint near him and beginning to work on the miniature goblin's sword. "It's a funny thing, to put so much time into goblins for a fighting game," he said after a moment, watching surreptitiously to gauge Wat's reaction.

Wat shook his head. "It's a game of choice. And seeing someone that *actually* looks like you is a joy I'm not sure humans could fully appreciate." He paused, grimacing. "Or the pain of seeing a line of shoddy miniatures, and knowing that's how you see us in combat as well."

By the time they met, Wat was already retired from military service, and that part of his life tended to be a blank in the history Lock knew, only revealed by Wat's severe limp and the amount of time he spent on these combat miniatures.

"Old habits, Wat. People don't like being uncomfortable."

"Let them choke on their own bile, then," Wat snorted. "Cor, most of 'em would rather we were still in the Lower Districts. If they really had a problem, they could let us out of serving when we want to go, 'stead of waiting for us to get too old, or too hurt, to fight."

Before Lock could reply, someone pounded on the door in the adjacent room. "Open up!" a muffled voice yelled. "Royals' business!"

Wat stared a moment, drew his knife from his belt, and walked to the door. "What Royals' business?" he yelled. "Who is it?"

The pounding stopped. "Is that Lieutenant Wat?" the voice said, much more quietly.

"Asked you the question, berk," Wat responded, shifting into the goblin slang he used when dealing with people in more direct ways ... though Lock noticed him start ever so slightly at the word *Lieutenant*. "What's the business?"

"Urgent, Sir. It's about the Captain."

Wat's eyes narrowed, and he looked at Lock, who was now standing nearby, listening intently. Lock nodded. "Stand clear of the door," Wat said, then drew the two locking bolts and opened the door quickly, knife at the ready. Standing on the other side, immediately saluting when he saw Wat, was a smaller goblin with a serious expression, dressed in red and gold livery with a shield slung on his back. "Mackey, Sir."

"Mackey," Wat said with a tight nod. "What about the Captain?"

Mackey fidgeted. "He—that is—" He shook his head. "We need you to come look at him, Lieutenant. He's unconscious. And . . . he might die."

※

Less than five minutes later, Lock, Wat, and Mackey were bumping along inside a carriage banging its way down Cable Street, the driver yelling at pedestrians and other slower coaches to get out of the way. "No one knew anything until about an hour ago," Mackey was saying. "I was on my way in, and just gotten off the stop in back of the barracks when I heard a yell from upstairs. I ran round to the front, and—"

"Why the front?" Lock interrupted.

Mackey grimaced as the carriage jolted once again over the uneven streets. "There's no door in the back, Sir—one to the side, but that's locked, and the regular entrance in the front."

"Then how did you hear the yell?"

"Through the window, a small one on the back wall of the building. Heard it loud and clear, so I ran—went right up to the second floor and inside the Captain's quarters. The door was already open, and Lieutenant Kirn was there, kneeling by the body of Captain Emson on the floor. He was conscious, but barely breathing. Had his hand on his chest, he did." Mackey shuddered.

"Why didn't you send for someone closer?" Wat asked, glaring. "Plenty of medics still in the service."

"He . . . requested it. The Captain. Said only you." Mackey

lowered his head. "Then he fainted, and Lieutenant Kirn told me to find you and get you here no matter what it took."

Wat leaned back, barely flinching as a particularly big jolt shook the carriage. Lock looked out the window of the carriage, which was beginning to slow down as it approached a wide, two-story building, the red and gold flag of the Third Division of the Cannisian Royals hanging above the front door.

Mackey led them past the guards and up the stairs to the second floor. Wat hurried into the room with Mackey, but Lock hesitated, looking down the long hallway toward a small window at its opposite end. After a moment, he walked quickly down the hall and looked through the closed window to the outside, then at the window's inside rim, where he saw a handle turned midway toward the unlocked position. He stared at the handle, then turned and headed back to Captain Emson's quarters.

Just inside the room, Mackey was talking in low tones to another goblin wearing the red and gold accented dress uniform of an officer, and as Lock came in, Mackey turned to face him. "Lieutenant Kirn, this is an investigator with—"

Kirn waved off the introduction impatiently. "I know who he is, Mackey. Back to your post; I'll manage from here." The private blinked, then saluted and exited the room as Kirn shook his head. "As if I wouldn't know the most famous investigator in Cannis. It's an honor, Sir."

Lock bowed slightly. "It's my pleasure, Lieutenant. But I'm only here as Wat's friend, of course, not in any official capacity."

"Still, it's appreciated." Kirn turned, and behind him Lock saw a simple wood-framed bed, Wat kneeling next to it. On the mattress lay what had to be Captain Emson, a goblin of middle-years, short-cropped grayish hair at his temples, hands by his sides. His eyes were closed, and Lock could see he was breathing... barely.

Lock walked to the bed and kneeled next to Wat, who had his head down on Emson's bared chest, an intent expression on his face. Wat lifted his head slowly. "He's in a bad way. Breathing shallow, heart irregular. Not much I can do for him, either... in this state, I doubt he'd survive the shock of surgery." He looked at Emson, whose dark eyebrows accented his unnaturally pale face.

"Was it a heart attack?" Lock asked.

"Could be," Wat said after a long moment, frowning. "But..." He trailed off, his frown darkening to a scowl, before glancing up at Lieutenant Kirn. "Kirn, could you give us a few moments?" Kirn raised an eyebrow but said nothing, simply nodding before turning to leave.

"You don't believe it?" Lock said as soon as Kirn was gone.

Wat looked at Lock, eyes narrowed. "No," he said in a low growl. "No, I don't. Emson could outrun most of the privates in the Third without breaking a sweat. Not to say we always see a heart attack coming, but it doesn't feel right."

"Right?"

Wat's face was grim. "Heart attacks aren't the only way someone goes down like this."

Lock nodded slowly. "Poison?"

"Maybe." Wat glanced around the room. "But from where? It's all... peaceful." Lock leaned over the bed, bending close to Emson's body. Where the captain's dress uniform shirt had been unbuttoned, Lock could see the gray hairs on his dark green chest as it rose and fell rapidly . . . and, around Emson's neck, a small oval locket, made of cunningly woven silver and gold. "No one else is even allowed up here, and . . ." Wat saw Lock peering at Emson's neck. "What?"

Lock did not reply. Instead, he squeezed the locket between his thumb and forefinger, and watched as the spring-loaded front opened. Inside was a portrait of a young female goblin, no more than six or seven years old. She was not smiling, but her deep brown eyes were wide and innocent, her face untroubled by time or disappointment. He gazed at it a long time before finally speaking again. "Where does Emson's family live?"

Wat blinked, looking surprised. "Emson doesn't have a family. Never talked about having one, anyway." He rose and came around to the other side of the bed. "Who is that? The paint's not old."

"Then I have to assume this is his daughter," Lock replied.

Wat looked at the picture more closely. "Same color eyes, same shape to the ears. Could be." He leaned back, his expression thoughtful. "He never mentioned her. Someone will need to find her to let her know what's happened . . . it'll be hard to track her down, though . . ." He trailed off as he saw Lock still looking at the portrait. "All right—what is it?"

Lock raised an eyebrow.

"Whenever you look at anything for that long," Wat said, "you've got an idea in your head. Then you talk about something else until I forget about it, and then, suddenly, back it comes as the explanation for everything."

"I look at everything, Wat. It's what I see that really matters."

"All right, then," Wat said, sounding exasperated. "So what do you see?"

Lock shook his head as he closed the locket, laid it back down on Emson's chest, and stood up. "I'm not sure yet."

"Excuse me," someone said from the door, and Lock and Wat looked up to see Lieutenant Kirn. "My apologies, but I wanted to check in on the Captain."

"No change," Wat replied.

"But it's good you're back, Lieutenant," Lock said. "I have a question for you." Kirn straightened as Lock walked around the bed to face him. "What is your relationship with Captain Emson?"

"He's my commanding officer."

"Your personal relationship, Lieutenant."

Kirn hesitated. "I respect him and follow orders. That's all that matters."

"Actually, it isn't all that matters, in this case," Lock replied. "If he wasn't your commanding officer, could you imagine him as a friend?"

Kirn set his jaw. "I don't see how that's any of your business, Sir."

"For Firx's sake, Kirn, we've got an officer down," Wat snapped. "Answer the question."

"The Captain asked for you, Wat," Kirn replied, raising his voice in turn. "Just you."

"That's right, berk, the Captain asked for me," Wat snarled as he stood, "and you were happy to see my investigator friend until he asked a question. Now, go on." Wat jerked his head in Lock's direction.

Kirn's jaw worked, but eventually his gaze dropped underneath Wat's withering glare. "No," he mumbled, voice sullen. "I wouldn't consider him a friend."

Lock nodded. "I see."

Suddenly Kirn looked up again, his expression fierce. "He wasn't kind, but he was fair, and I did respect him. Everyone did. When I came in and found him . . ." He paused. "No one would want to see him like this," he finally finished after a long silence.

"All right, Lieutenant," Lock said. "Please don't go far; you may be needed." Kirn swallowed and gave a tight nod before turning on his heel and striding out of the room, where Lock could hear him bellowing orders as he marched back down the stairs. Lock looked for quite a while at the open door. "Wat," he finally said. "What's the procedure when a soldier dies in Cannis?"

Wat frowned. "What do you mean, 'procedure'?"

"I mean, what happens to them? Do they get a state funeral, a ceremony, interment at the city graveyard, that kind of thing?"

"Depends on the kind of soldier," Wat said, sourly.

"Officer or enlisted, you mean?"

Wat grunted. "Human or goblin." Lock turned to stare at him. "Don't act so surprised, Lock. You know as well as I do that Cannis is two cities mashed together, even now, one doing its best to consume the other. We die for the Royals; we still die without respect."

"Then what's the procedure?"

"If a human soldier dies, they're given a simple funeral at city expense as soon as possible. Officer or enlisted, the process is the same."

"And if it's a goblin?"

"If it's proven—usually by the division commander, but sometimes the family has to make the appeal directly—that the goblin was killed in the line of duty, they get the same thing, more or less. But if the poor sod just keels over on the street, or goes of his injuries . . ."

"He doesn't get the funeral?"

Wat nodded angrily. "He's taken away by a special crew, humans only, within the Royals. For years no one knew what happened to them after that. But I had a friend off duty once, who saw that crew with the body of a goblin soldier. My friend got curious, and he followed them outside the city walls. Stupid thing to do, really . . . if he got caught he'd have been drummed out of the Royals, possibly jailed or even executed. But he stayed quiet, and they never saw him." Wat sighed, his gaze growing distant. "He followed them all the way to a swamp outside Cannis. And there . . ." Wat's nostrils flared. "They dumped him. Tossed the body into the muck, then left. No ceremony, or song, or even a word. Just tossed and forgotten." Suddenly Wat looked up at Lock, his gaze refocused. "Heard the letter they sent the wife and son was fancy, though."

Lock nodded slowly, watching the war between anger and sadness on Wat's face, before the larger goblin turned away. "Why do you care so much about the fate of goblin soldiers anyway, Lock?" he asked, voice husky. "Seeing one dying make it real?"

"I'm sorry," Lock said. "It wasn't a question I would have thought to ask, until it became relevant, as it is now."

Wat turned back. "What do you mean?"

Lock put his hands behind his back and straightened. "Your diagnosis, Doctor. What happened to Captain Emson?"

Wat hesitated, looking back at the bed. "I'd say he suffered a major heart event, causing him to slip into a coma. Best guess is he's done for."

"But not from natural causes?" Lock asked, walking back to the bed and gazing down at Captain Emson.

"Can I prove it? No. But given his medical history and health, I'd say not. My assumption is that the conditions for this heart event were created artificially."

"Poison."

Wat hesitated before replying. "Yes."

"How long would it take for such a poison to take effect?"

"Depends, but probably a few minutes."

"So it was done here."

Anger had won again in Wat's expression. "Sure, could have been Kirn." He looked at the door through which Kirn had exited. "Hate to think it, but he had the time to do it, and at least some motive . . . set himself up for obvious promotion to commander of the Third. More likely an unnoticed visitor, from a rival division, maybe. Maybe one of them got paid off by a human officer who doesn't like how well our units are fighting for Cannis, wants to knock them down a few pegs." He began to pace back and forth. "We'll never prove a thing."

"Wat," Lock said quietly, reaching down to the locket around Emson's neck and picking it up again, the smooth metal cold in the palm of his hand.

"What does that blasted locket have to do with anything?" Wat asked angrily. "You've been obsessed with—"

"Can a substance," Lock interrupted, "mimic the effects of a poison—without leading to death? Something which leaves the body on its own, after a period of time?"

Wat's mouth, clearly opened to prepare for another salvo, snapped shut as the goblin's eyes widened. "Well—obviously," he finally managed. "Sallic root, rishin extract, a few others. Why?"

Lock laid the locket back down on Emson's chest, tilted his head and leaned down, putting his right ear directly above Emson's mouth. "His breath is shallow, but regular." He put his head on Emson's chest. "His heartbeat's irregular, yes, but not fluttering. It's mostly just slow." He straightened up again as Wat, a frustrated expression on his face, came over and leaned in to listen.

After a minute Wat stood up. "Yes, I suppose. It's an odd rhythm, like one in between life and death."

"I agree. And unless I miss my guess, I think Captain Emson would want to choose life." Wat stared at him. "No one poisoned your Captain, Wat," Lock went on, "unless your Captain poisoning himself counts. But then, this isn't really poison." He walked to the door and looked out to see a goblin in red and gold guarding the room to the left, the window at the end of the hallway to the right. "That window," he said as he turned back, "is on the other end of a long hallway, and these walls are thick as barricades. If I yelled as loudly as I could—if you and I both yelled together—the guard outside this room would hear us, and maybe someone on the same floor, a room or two down. But I doubt anyone on the first floor would hear us, and certainly not anyone outside the building. A cry from inside this room wouldn't draw anyone's notice."

Wat's eyes widened. "So the cry Mackey heard—"

"—came from right next to the window, which I saw is still half-unlocked," Lock finished. "Assuming that Emson was the one making the sound, he was by the window when he did it."

"Maybe he knew he was in trouble . . . went to the window, yelled for help . . ."

"If he had that strength, why not go down the stairs and out the front door instead, where any number of passersby could have helped him?"

Wat's jaw worked. "Then Mackey was lying about hearing the yell."

"It's possible," Lock admitted. "But Mackey came in off the Third Division stop, as he likely does every day."

"A conspiracy, then? Kirn and Mackey working together?"

"Possible. Except that they sent for you. If they wanted Emson dead, why not finish the job they started, then call the local doctor, probably a human? The doctor certifies the death, Emson's body is bagged and carted, and any suspicion passes quickly . . . especially for a goblin from the Third."

Wat pursed his lips. "I never did like thinking of the crew doing it. But the Captain wanted me here for a reason . . ."

"He did." Lock touched the locket again. "Imagine, Wat, a good commander; a good leader, tough but fair, respected if not loved by all of his troops. Imagine if that goblin first took a position in the military out of need . . . and then, to his own surprise, is successful, then promoted, all the way to the top of the chain.

But he's under constant pressure from superior officers, all human, who will never consider him anything more than a goblin, bound to be less trustworthy, to make mistakes. And something—someone—waits for him outside the city walls." He opened the locket to reveal the picture of the young goblin. "Yet, as a goblin, he's not at liberty to leave until an injury does it for him."

Wat's glare intensified, but he said nothing.

"Then he ensures someone who knows him, a medic who served under him in the past, who won't just accept that he's keeled over and died, is ready to be summoned when the time comes . . . to confirm his 'death.'"

"What are you . . . ?" Wat began before trailing off.

"Suppose Emson doesn't want to die, but he *does* want to leave the Third and Cannis. If any other doctor comes to examine him, a valuable asset to the Royals, they 'save' him, he recovers—and he stays as Captain, and stays in Cannis with the Third, and nothing has changed."

"But I examined him, and eventually I'd have saved him too," Wat objected.

"Yes. He needed someone who thinks non-medically. And he knew you'd bring me with you. And more than perhaps anyone else in Cannis, you already know what it means to be a good soldier, and an honorable one . . . and a tired one, too, missing one's family."

Wat rubbed his chin absently. "So long as I lie, and certify a death that hasn't happened. Spare one of the good linen bags, for an officer . . ."

"Yes—a request which would be denied, since in this

scenario, he poisoned himself," Lock said. "Instead, he's removed from the city, by a special crew. Humans only." Wat stared at Lock as he continued. "A gamble. But it's a good gamble, because Emson knew that whatever decision you would make would be an honorable one."

The doctor stared at the locket, into the deep, haunting gaze of the young goblin girl. Then he turned and walked to the door. "Kirn," he shouted. "We have some things to discuss."

"Wat," Lock said. Wat glanced over his shoulder. "The friend who followed that special crew of the Royals to the swamp. How well did you know him?"

Wat held Lock's gaze for a long time. "About as well as I know myself," he said finally, then departed.

Lock smiled and closed his eyes. Somewhere in his imagination, he saw a cart rolling away from a lonely swamp, a wound in the earth into which bodies would sink and decay. Yet one body stirred, drew breath, almost choking on the fetid air. But the breath was enough, and the living goblin rolled away from the dead, crawled slowly back to the solidness of ground. There he would wait, gathering strength, feeling the breeze on his skin, out of armor and uniform for the first time in years. Then he would rise and set his steps away from the swamp and Cannis, and feel every step growing lighter as he went, each one leading him over hill and under star to a village, and a young goblin woman with deep brown eyes running toward him, arms flung wide in welcome.

Gregory A. Wilson is Professor of English at St. John's University, where he teaches creative writing and speculative fiction, and is author of Clemson UP's *The Problem in the Middle: Liminal Space and the Court Masque*, book chapters, and journal articles. Outside academia he is author of the epic fantasy *The Third Sign*; the award-winning graphic novel *Icarus;* and dark fantasies *Grayshade, Renegade,* and *Heretic*; and the 5E adventure/sourcebook *Tales and Tomes from the Forbidden Library*; plus many short stories. Under the moniker Arvan Eleron he runs a Twitch channel about narrative, with many sponsored TTRPG campaigns. His website is gregoryawilson.com.

Hands Are for Helping
Sarah Hans

Tonya's new one-bedroom basement apartment was dark and damp. There was no stove or refrigerator, but it was all she could afford, with no down payment and no job, only the meager assistance offered by the charitable organizations helping families displaced by the fire. She had managed to get some furniture from friends, a futon and an old dresser and a bookcase, a few tatty blankets, some hand-me-down clothes in Neo's size. At a church garage sale, she'd snagged a small fridge/freezer combo like the kind people used in dorms and a hot pot for heating water, both filthy but serviceable once they were cleaned.

People were generally sympathetic to her situation, though many gave Tonya side-eye that told her they secretly thought she was a monster. What else do you call someone who leaves their child alone all day, locked into an apartment that became a death trap when the ancient wiring couldn't handle his new computer?

All it took was one phone call from the social worker and a new system was sent over, pronto, installed with a single plug and the flip of a switch. The kiosk lurked in a corner of the single room, its shiny, clean plastic and glass a sharp counterpoint to the hazy shadows of the basement apartment.

Tonya fantasized about destroying it. While Neo curled

gratefully in her lap, his arms wrapped so tightly around her waist he nearly stole her breath, she wept to the social worker. "I want Neo to go to a real school. Putting him in front of a screen hasn't been good for him."

The social worker, a middle-aged white woman who had no children of her own, patted Tonya's hand. "Many kids—especially boys—start having behavior problems around this age. The good thing is that now he has a therapist, and the doctor has prescribed him some medication, so he ought to be doing much better very soon."

"He doesn't need a therapist or medication. He needs to go to a real school. It's not natural for a six-year-old to sit in front of a screen all day."

"He's on the waiting list for the Haverford School—"

Tonya sucked her teeth and hugged her boy closer, thinking of the School of the Future, Neo's last school. Rows of computers with children in front of them, swinging their legs in the too-tall chairs, a class of fifty kindergarteners attended by a bored woman who barely looked twenty years old. It hadn't been good enough for any child, and she'd been unable to afford the tuition with her daycare-teacher salary. "That's just like the School of the Future, only worse. I have friends who send their kids there. They can hardly read, and there's a lot of fighting."

The social worker sighed. "Well, there's always home-schooling."

"I didn't go to college." Tonya bit back against the regret that threatened to overwhelm her, dashing away thoughts of the nursing career she'd given up to follow Neo's father to this city where she knew no one, only to become pregnant and, then, alone. "I don't have the money for homeschooling classes and exams. And how am I supposed to work a job if I can't send my son to school, but I can't leave him alone, either?"

The social worker's phone buzzed. She checked the screen briefly, brightened, and stood to go. "You're doing everything right. I know you'll get this figured out. Just hang in there, and I'll be around to check on you next week."

After the social worker left, Tonya let her son cling to her, rocking him back and forth while she stroked his soft hair. She murmured the lullaby she used to sing to him when he was an infant. They'd only been apart three months, but she'd swear on a Bible he'd grown in that short time, and now she wondered if the clothes she'd collected would even fit him. She wanted to ask him about foster care, about whether his foster parents had really been as good to him as the social worker claimed, but she swallowed the question. She'd let him tell her about it in his own time. She wasn't sure she could bear hearing about it, anyway. If the foster family had been horrible to him, she'd be upset he'd been taken from her and traumatized. If the foster family had been wonderful, she'd feel jealous and hurt, wondering whether some other family wouldn't give Neo a better life than living in a dark basement, sharing a futon with his mom and learning from artificial intelligence in front of a screen all day.

Better to leave it alone.

A few hours after the social worker left, Tonya's friend Iris arrived with her cousin Lawrence. Tonya fidgeted with anxiety as Lawrence crouched under the computer kiosk. Neo lay a few feet away on the bed, watching videos on Iris's phone with its unlimited-data plan while Lawrence hacked the virtual tutor, and Iris visited with Tonya.

"Are you sure this is legal?" Tonya asked, chewing a patch of dry skin on her lower lip.

"Totally legal," Iris said. "I don't know anybody who's been caught, anyway, and even if you were, they'd probably just lock the system down again. What are they going to do? All kids are guaranteed a free education. They can't take it away."

From a few feet away, Lawrence said, "This is like selling your food stamps. They expect you to do it. Otherwise, they wouldn't make it so easy."

"Be grateful for small favors, I guess," Tonya said, her stomach churning with unease.

Iris helped her sign up with Funglish, a site where Tonya would teach English to kids in other countries via the internet. As she set up the space according to the Funglish specifications and signed up for late-night timeslots when Neo would be sleeping, she burned with resentment. Why were kids in other countries entitled to an actual, human teacher while her own son was not? Why were kids in other countries entitled to her time when her own son was only guaranteed time with a virtual tutor? She ate an entire box of Twinkies after Neo fell asleep, trying to quell her rage and despair.

She woke in the morning to Neo standing over her with a bowl of cereal and a spoon. "Morning, Mama! I made you breakfast," he chirped, grinning proudly.

Tonya pulled Neo into her embrace and smothered him with

kisses, so grateful to be reunited with her boy, she didn't mind the milk sloshing over the side of the bowl onto the floor. They spent the morning eating until they felt sick, snuggled up under the covers watching silly videos on the hacked computer. Tonya inhaled the scent of her son's skin and promised herself she'd be more grateful for these moments instead of dwelling on the unfairness she could do nothing about.

In the afternoon, Neo signed onto the virtual tutor. While he worked on his lessons, Tonya bustled around the tiny apartment, trying to keep busy. She made them both ramen noodles for dinner when it was time. Then she reluctantly put Neo back on the computer for another hour of lessons, so he would meet his daily quota. With Children's Services on her back, she couldn't afford to let him miss any time. He argued and fought her, but she got him to agree to finish his time by making them both hot chocolate with marshmallows—his favorite.

Neo settled in and pulled on his headphones, his wide eyes reflecting the image of Humphrey the dragon dancing on the screen. Humphrey was small, blue, and adorable, a creature made of round shapes, with huge eyes and a big, friendly smile. Even through the headphones, Tonya could hear the first strains of the song, "Hands Are for Helping," and she cringed. It was a sweet song about being kind but, damn, was it annoying. She went to the small, high window, the only one the basement apartment afforded her, and stood, looking out. She thought about going to the corner store for some magazines to read, but she didn't have the money for magazines, and she was nervous about her first Funglish lessons anyway, which were in only a few hours. She missed having a real cell phone with a data plan, so she could get on the internet when she was bored, instead of this prepaid garbage. She tried to savor her hot chocolate and gazed out at her new neighborhood at ankle height.

The sidewalk was mostly abandoned. Someone in Converse walked past, and a few minutes later, walked back with a plastic bag full of groceries from the corner store. A pair of old work boots clomped into the building. Tonya sipped her drink, letting her mind wander. She recalled the small, warm classroom where she'd attended kindergarten, where they'd played in a tiny kitchen, dressed up in clothes from a magical trunk, and clapped along to songs sung by a cheerful, bright-eyed teacher. Before public education had been reduced to a plastic box and a screen with an animated dragon.

Neo hummed along with the song, adorably off-key, his chair squeaking as he kicked his legs in time to the music.

A car pulled into the parking space right in front of Tonya's window, a blue Honda with a bumper so low it scraped the curb. A woman's dress shoes and ankles emerged from the driver's side, followed by a little girl's light-up sneakers. The girl dropped a tablet on the ground as she emerged from the car and her mother scolded her, just audible through the glass. Tonya could see the girl's hair was braided into tidy cornrows capped with shiny beads when she bent over to pick up the device. Humphrey the dragon's familiar blue form gyrated on the tablet screen.

Mother and daughter moved to the sidewalk, the girl's eyes locked on the screen, her mother's hand practically dragging her, a familiar sight. Tonya sipped her hot chocolate.

The girl suddenly yanked her wrist from her mother's grasp. Her knees buckled, and she collapsed to the ground. She convulsed, thrashing rigidly, foaming at the mouth. The tablet slid from her fingers, and Tonya got a flash of Humphrey the blue dragon, but there was something wrong with him. His body was pixelated, his eyes a piercing yellow, and he made weird, twisting shapes, jerking and jumping unnaturally, much like the girl did on the sidewalk. She could hear the song faintly through the glass now, but it didn't sound right, either. Like it had been corrupted, broken up, replayed in a minor key, and remixed by someone who wrote scores for horror movies.

Tonya dropped her mug to the floor with a thud, hot liquid spilling across her bare toes.

Neo continued bouncing in his chair while Humphrey extolled the virtues of using your fingers to share toys and hold hands instead of using them for violence. The mother outside the window pulled her seizing daughter into her lap and screamed for help, the sound agonizing, making Tonya's hair stand on end. White-hot dread lanced through her chest, stealing her breath.

She yanked the headphones from Neo's head and tried to cover his eyes with her hand.

Neo shouted in surprise, "Mama, what?"

Tonya pulled him from the chair and wrapped her arms around him. "Don't look at it, baby. Don't listen!" He wrapped his arms around her neck and his legs around her waist like he did when he was a timid toddler, and Tonya fought with the kiosk, punching buttons as Humphrey elongated, unraveling, his mouth opening too wide. The song still issuing from the headphones took on a menacing timbre. "How do I turn it off?"

Neo pointed to the power cord that snaked from the kiosk to the nearby outlet, and Tonya grabbed for it, the computer going dark as the plug exited the wall socket. The song cut off abruptly, and Humphrey's corrupted gyrations went black. Tonya's ears were full of her own thundering pulse and raspy, panicked breathing.

She plopped Neo onto the futon. "Stay there." She went to the toolbox buried in the closet and found the hammer. With a scream of triumph, she drove the hammer into the kiosk, shattering the screen, scattering the keys from the keyboard. She focused on the center of the kiosk, where she suspected the hard drive was hidden, and as the plastic shell cracked and fell away with a few more swings of her hammer, she reached in and jerked out as many wires as she could, ignoring the way the shards of plastic sliced into her fingers.

When the thing had been thoroughly destroyed, she stood back and appreciated her handiwork for a moment.

Outside, the mother on the sidewalk screamed, a miserable howl of loss and pain.

Dropping the hammer, Tonya reminded Neo to stay put and went outside. She fished her phone out of her pocket to call 9-1-1, but when she arrived beside the woman, a cell phone was already out and lying on the sidewalk, the screen brightly lit and displaying the emergency numbers.

The mother looked up at Tonya and screamed, "Why is nobody coming? They've put me on hold. My baby is dying, and they've put me on hold!" Snot bubbled from her nose, and her face scrunched up in agony as she bent over her little girl, her body convulsing with sobs.

In the distance, tires screeched and horns blared. Tonya winced. Screaming voices raised into the afternoon air. Sirens seemed like they were wailing all over the city. Overhead, a helicopter thumped past. With a feeling of horror tingling behind her breastbone, Tonya realized this event was not isolated to Neo and this little girl.

It was happening all over the city. Maybe all over the state.

Her gaze on the sky, Tonya swore she saw something blue gyrating and glinting behind the clouds, something unthinkably huge and menacing, something twirling and twitching just far enough out of the atmosphere so that it was barely visible to the naked eye. She shook her head to clear it of the hallucination and knelt by the girl. She pressed her fingers into the child's neck, desperately seeking a pulse, and found herself humming the irritating chorus for "Hands Are for Helping."

A few weeks later, Tonya and Neo arrived at the home of their first client. Neo loved to carry the big pink bag his mom had purchased to carry the supplies she needed for her new career, including a copy of the emergency certification she'd earned in the last few weeks that gave her clearance to do the work. She double-checked the apartment number and knocked.

A woman opened the door. Her black hair was pulled into

a messy bun, and there were three old scratches healing on her cheek. She looked on the verge of tears. "Yes?"

Tonya offered her hand in greeting. "Mrs. Reyes? I'm Tonya Baker. It's nice to meet you."

Mrs. Reyes breathed a heavy sigh as they shook hands. "I'm so glad you're here. Please, call me Jasmine." Her eyes went to Neo. "Is this your son?"

Neo nodded proudly and stuck out his own hand to shake, just as his mother had taught him to do. "Hello, ma'am, I'm Neo."

Jasmine's eyes grew huge, and she looked at Tonya. "He's not...?"

"No, ma'am. We were lucky." Tonya stroked her son's hair and smiled. Of course, Neo was supposed to be in school, but Tonya cared very little for the government's rules right now. If some bureaucrat showed up to lecture her or take her son away, they were going to suffer the full force of her rage and a letter from a lawyer. The massive class action lawsuit against the state and federal education agencies had ensured everyone was busy with that anyway, so she was pretty sure she'd fly under their radar. And, of course, they were also busy creating a new program for the kiosks, a program that would, supposedly, reverse the damage that had been done on that terrible day almost two months ago.

But, of course, few parents trusted the virtual tutor to undo the situation it had created. And how do you use a kiosk to teach an unresponsive child who has violent seizures triggered by bright lights and loud noises? So, the government had created emergency certification training to train people who had experience working with kids to help them.

There was little proof the system would work, but it was better than doing nothing. And it was a steady government paycheck, with benefits and the fulfillment of helping people, which was all Tonya had ever really wanted out of her aborted nursing degree.

Tonya turned back to her client. "We should get started. We don't want to waste any of your time."

Jasmine nodded and ushered them inside. On the couch sat a girl, maybe eight years old, staring glassy-eyed at the television. She looked like a miniature version of her mother. She was wearing an adult's long-sleeved shirt with her arms in the sleeves and the sleeves tied behind her back, a makeshift straitjacket. She didn't look up when new people entered her home. Drool oozed from her mouth and down her chin.

"She's like this most of the day," her mother whimpered. "The TV keeps her calm." She gestured helplessly to the scabs healing on the girl's cheeks. Jasmine's eyes, when she looked up at Tonya, brimmed with desperation. "Who did this to our kids? The Russians? The Chinese? I heard maybe it was one of our own people, a disgruntled programmer—"

"I'm sorry," Tonya said. "But I don't know. That wasn't part of the training." As she said it, she couldn't help thinking about the enormous blue shape flashing and twisting in the sky overhead, above the clouds, higher than an airplane. She still had dreams about Humphrey the dragon and the irritating song that had turned into that strange, haunting, stilted sort of pink noise issuing from her son's headphones. *Hands are for helping.* She shuddered.

Jasmine looked away, frowning.

"It's alright," Tonya told her, martialing herself and nodding at Neo. "We're here now. It will take time, but we'll get your daughter back. Now, what's her name?"

"Ella."

Neo carried the bag of supplies to the couch and perched beside the girl as if nothing were wrong, as if he were on a playdate. A few strands of hair had slipped from Ella's ponytail, and he brushed them from her face, tucking them gently behind her ear. "Hi, Ella," he said, smiling. He reached for the remote control and switched off the television. The girl blinked.

"I'm Neo. We're going to be friends."

Sarah Hans is an award-winning writer, editor, and teacher whose stories have appeared in more than 40 publications, including *Apex Magazine* and *Pseudopod*. Her latest projects are a horror novella titled *Asylum* and her second short fiction collection, *Chorus of Whispers*. She lives in Ohio with her partner, an amazing kid, more pets than she can afford, and enough craft supplies to keep her busy for the next 200 years.

All the Light in the Room
GABRIELLE HARBOWY

1. Alderidge

You may consider the foot soldiers unremarkable: eight pieces per side, cast from the same mold, whose role is to die for the strategy of the game. It is not so. The foot soldiers require bravery, loyalty . . . even seeds of martyr hood. Finding them is my favorite part. This is why my sets are better than Rhodes's.

Rhodes uses the disabled for his foot soldiers—and still calls them foot*men*. Two practices that he knows offend me, but that, too, may be part of why Rhodes does it. He believes those who have disadvantages have built stronger spirits to overcome them. He also believes men are stronger at the core than other people because of the advantages that make them so. He does not see the contradiction between these two views. He never will.

My white eye and my clawed hand, and my lack of affinity with any gender, do not give me magical insight or strength of will. It is an insult to say so. They only bring out the true nature of the people around me, and that is not magic. There is nothing magic about pettiness.

I digress. You asked: "Why me?" And I am answering.

Look at your medals. You display them so proudly, these

mementos of a war from a dead century. And look at you now, alone, lacking purpose. I will reunite you with your medals, melt you and reform you, and set you guard over eternal wars where your sacrifice will make a difference long after we are all dust.

Now quickly, before the drug sets in: which of these medals do you want to be a part of you, and which should I leave for burial with your remains? Excellent. There's a good, old lad.

Merelle joins me in the workshop, while I grind down the axe that took the groundskeeper's life, building him into a small mountain of bloodied metal flakes. She kisses me, *oohs* and *aahs* over the man's medals, and kisses me again. She recognizes them. She too has served in war.

A decade ago, she would have asked if such a decorated find would not be better placed as a rook or a knight, but by now, she trusts my insight. Just as I trust hers, when she chooses her wood to construct the field for my pieces' eternal battle.

Each weapon is only used once. One sacrifice's blood. It is murder, yes, what my brother Rhodes and I do. But it grants immortality. And in a way, it's the perfect crime: destroy the weapon, and it can never be found. Make art of it, and the soul adds value to the world forever.

The flakes are in the crucible, and now I grind down the medal to join them. Goggles, their lenses thick and tinted; gloves, stained with soot and lives; apron, thick leather worn rough in some places, and in others worn smooth. With these all secured,

I heat the metal pieces and watch them cohere, forming a silvery lake that turns orange hot. Then comes the casting. Pouring out the lake into a fine ribbon no hand may touch, filling the mold, making the pawn. Quenching. Polishing. Already, I feel the power from this one when I turn it in my hands. I put this final pawn beside the rest. They resonate together, a hum I can feel in my teeth and behind my eyes. It is good.

"Purpleheart and bloodwood," Merelle says, inspecting the pieces.

"Oh! Exotic choices, Professor Knoll," I answer. I cannot see what she sees. She must feel the power that I do, but in her own way.

"I think this is the one," she says quietly, sliding her arm around my waist. "The final one. The pinnacle of everything."

Yes. The pinnacle. That feeling was inside me too, but I had not attached the word to it.

"All our work," I answer. Her hair frames her face in short silver curls, even more beautiful now in their winter than when they were chestnut and golden and all shades of autumn. Her eyes are still deep, almost black, like an icy pond at night.

"Best get about it then, Professor Claremont." Those eyes twinkle, reflecting her grin.

2. Cosima

When Iris's light went out, *all* the lights on campus went out.

Iris, my roommate, was a voice major. She could do pop and jazz and choir and whatever, but she was training for opera. Mezzo, not too deep and not too shrill, one of those voices that gets right under your skin and makes all your hair stand up and tingle on your arms. A voice you wanted to swim in, not caring if you drowned. But you wouldn't, because some gleam in her eye would catch you just in time and float you back to shore.

We knew she lit up every room she entered, but we knew it figuratively. Not until she died did we realize it was a literal thing, too.

But it was okay, in the end because that was how we caught them.

Darkgrove School of the Arts was a gorgeous gothic campus with sprawling grounds. I developed my passion for piano there, and was the go-to accompanist for many of my classmates, including Iris. I loved the challenge of sight-reading and the symbiosis, the *synergy*, of performing with someone else and guiding them, getting to the soaring highs and the triumph of the final measures together. And sometimes, I felt something in that synergy. Some energy that came from me, that came *through* me, to do more than my simple playing ever could.

Which is why, maybe, I was extra devastated when I came home from the practice rooms to find Iris beyond my help. Bleeding out. In the dark.

The door to our room had been open, but that wasn't unusual. You left your door open a crack when you weren't doing much, to signal it was okay for friends to visit unannounced. I still knocked before I opened it fully. Was surprised when I didn't see her. Was more surprised when I did.

I knelt in her blood. There was so much of it, I had to wade into it to get close to her. And I screamed. And screamed. And people came with candles and flashlights and first aid kits and devices, and it didn't help. I couldn't help. Her light was already gone.

3. Alderidge

The knife is intimate, personal. It requires close quarters. To kill with a knife says: "You will feel my breath as you die."

It is risky, for certain, but I admit I have too much respect for you, Iris, to transform you in any lesser way. Your talent is more magical than you know. You will be the strongest queen to ever grace my boards. I assure you—it is an honor and a compliment. No, don't try to thrash.

Relax now. Soon, you'll own the spotlight forever.

In addition to being a tenured professor of sculpture, I also cosponsor the chess club, with my brother. Merelle, of course, uses her woodworking expertise to create the perfect boards for us. Rhodes and I display our handmade sets, but we also compete with them, and our students love to watch. Some gamble, though of course that's not encouraged. But consider: they live and breathe their work just as we do, and occasional recreation is just as important for them as it is for us, is it not?

This set will be my masterpiece. I can feel it.

I cast Iris's piece the same evening, working by candlelight and the brilliance of the forge. The lights all across campus went out when she died, but not all the electricity. Only the lights. A fitting tribute to a bright soul, it brought me nearly to tears then... and still does, to think about it. Oh, how perfect it will be.

The metal sweats and pools and begins to glow, the red of love and then the pure white of life. When I pour it, the glow lingers even as it cools. The queen, the brightest soul, the strength of the board. How powerful she will be, surrounded by the souls of warriors, lifted upon their shoulders. When I part the draperies around my bed and sink into its comfort, I dream of strength and light.

Sunday afternoon. Merelle returns from the groundskeeper's memorial service and unwraps her headscarf. I can feel the chill coming off the fabric, short-lived in the heat of the forge, but refreshing like a brief sip from a stream. We stand together silently, hand in hand.

The play is nearly cast. Only the king remains.

4. Cosima

When I met Iris, I wasn't a Darkgrove student yet. I hadn't even heard about the school until I met her, really.

We had both taken the same boy to our sophomore year homecoming dances—her, because he was a classmate and friend; me, because Max was my neighbor. We'd gone to Hebrew School together, and we had always been each other's dates to things, even once he went to a different high school. Because it was a boarding school, I assumed it was both really expensive and far out of state somewhere, not set back in the woods in the next county over.

At our dance, he told me about Iris. He said I'd like her, and we should meet. I got a ride up one weekend and the three of us hung out. It was magic. We jammed. We sang. We hiked. We improvised harmonies to the radio. We floated through the vaulted marble hallways like ghosts and posed in our goth finery in front of stone and ivy.

I committed to piano, even though it had never been more than a hobby, and transferred that same term. We were already making plans to room together the following semester.

Iris had been the one to clue me in on modeling for the visual arts departments in our spare time. Sculpting, woodworking, painting. It didn't matter. You stood or sat, either in a costume or in a skin-colored leotard (they didn't actually expect students to pose nude), for a couple of hours, and made maybe forty bucks.

Considering that, I wasn't surprised when some of the visual arts kids, and their professors, turned up at Iris's service. A couple of art students, I think, were actually sketching her casket. Max and I sat with Iris's mom on the awkward folding chairs, buffering her from all the folks expressing sorrow and telling her a bunch of empty words about her daughter that we knew she wasn't even hearing.

It was out in the quad, since the lights still weren't back on in the buildings. A black, canopy-tent thing had been erected over all of us. It didn't do much to keep the wind out or heat in, just left us all in a gloomy shadow despite the sunny day.

The visual arts professors expressed their sympathy as a group. The sculpting teachers, the Professors Claremont, were siblings, both pasty-skinned; Rhodes was a man, thinning salt-and-pepper hair, immaculate suit, a five-o'clock shadow that looked suave on him, not scruffy. Alderidge was nonbinary, and most people were happy to be able to call them Dr. or Professor as a way to sidestep the pronoun dance. It wasn't that they were completely androgynous, but more like gender was a dye that didn't stick to them. I was glad they taught there, honestly, because they were a lot of students' first exposure to nonbinary folks, you could tell, and learning how to navigate that sort of thing was as important as cleaning your brushes or practicing your scales. Alderidge was married to Professor Knoll, she taught wood sculpting, and she was with them too. After Dr. Claremont offered their good hand to shake Iris's mom's, she did the same. She had the kind of grandmotherly figure and warm eyes that made you want to ask her for a hug, and I nearly did, except that I wanted to stay strong for Iris's mom.

A young guy in maintenance overalls had put the flower arrangements out, and was now acting as usher. That was usually Mr. Percival's job, but the groundskeeper was old and slow these days, a veteran whose rough youth was catching up with him, so I wasn't surprised that a couple of people were saying that he'd quietly retired.

After the service, we packed up Iris's stuff, which had already been searched, photographed, and dusted, and loaded her mom's car. Max and I looked at each other in silence as she drove away.

"Want to go practice?" he asked.

I slid my finger behind the lens of my glasses and rubbed

under my eye, hoping my mascara had been as waterproof as advertised. I never wore the stuff. It was Iris's. "Is there light in the music building yet?"

"Oh. Right. Probably not. Between us, I bet we could wheel a piano out into the quad? There aren't *too* many stairs."

I smiled despite myself. "Hey, just grab some candles and your violin. For Iris, we'll make it work."

5. Alderidge

Oh, my beloved Merelle, don't cry. I'll be here with you always, under your hand. We always meant for me to be the final piece of our pinnacle board, tying the magic together with my own blood. Don't weep. You'll feel me near, and I'm certain I'll still feel you. Look at how much of their souls these other pieces retain. The pawns, so strong and able. The knights, so fierce and loyal. The rooks and bishops, ready to sacrifice themselves for others. The queen and the light that shines from within her. And I, I embrace the irony of the position of king. The ultimate gendered ruler, who unites the others together with a single purpose: to protect the one who made them.

I demanded sacrifice, and I cannot do so without demanding the same of myself.

And the crime, my crime, is the perfect crime. I alone am guilty of the creation of my pieces, and I will have ascended out of reach of mortal justice. The only judge who can sentence me will be the arbiter of the chess match.

Come now—the injection is taking hold of me. You know what to do. Make true with the strike. Grind the metal with the blood. You know what to do from there. Victory will be ours . . . together.

6. Cosima

A quiet search still continued for the murder weapon, but the killer had been careful. No weapon left behind, no footprints in the blood, no fingerprints, even on the door. The autopsy hadn't told Iris's mom anything we didn't already know, or at least she didn't tell us if it did. But why Iris? No one disliked her or had any kind of grudge. There hadn't been any kind of competition for roles. The killer had stolen nothing, except her light.

The floor had been cleaned professionally, so the room had New Dorm smell. With her stuff gone, the room was all mine. But it didn't feel like mine. It definitely didn't feel like ours.

At loose ends, I invited Max to the end-of-term chess tournament. It always started with a showcase game between the professors Claremont, using whatever masterpiece chess set they'd carved and sculpted over the semester. I wore a fancy black flapper dress with sequins and fringe, and a hairband to match. Max wore a three-piece suit and brought me a corsage of black roses, just like when we'd gone to school dances together.

Arm in arm, we joined the queue of students filing into the Visual Arts lecture auditorium. Glass lanterns lit the vast stone halls, casting shadows as much as light.

As was tradition, there was a procession that led past the masterwork board itself, everyone taking their turn to *ooh* and *aah* across the guide ropes before finding their seats.

They had outdone themselves this year. The inlaid wood

squares were purple and deep brownish red wood, all outlined in black. Small plaques noted that the pale reddish figures carved of marble—the "white" pieces—were the work of Rhodes Claremont. The "black" pieces Alderidge Claremont had cast were an odd black metal with a purple sheen, perfectly complementing the board, which of course had been made by Merelle Knoll.

It was all breathtakingly exquisite. I knew little to nothing about chess or sculpture, but the folds of cloth on the figures, the expressions on their faces, the leaves on their circlets, were all as vivid as life. In the flickering light, they seemed to move with their own consciousness.

Max and I moved along, aware of the queue behind us, and found seats toward the front. Once the line thinned out and the crowd started settling into creaking velvet seats, Max sat up suddenly, rubbing his eyes.

"Candle smoke getting to you?" I asked, leaning in to bump shoulders, to be heard above the din.

He shook his head. "Is it just me, or . . . That. On the board. Do you see that?"

I squinted. Now that there weren't bodies obscuring it, now that the flickering lights had settled, what I'd assumed was glare off my glasses, now that I scrutinized it . . . It could have been an effect, some sort of magic or trick of technology, the glow emanating from the chess board. But it was uneven. Only on one side.

I eased out of my seat, holding the cushion to try to keep it from squeaking as it folded back up. I expected Max to hiss at me to sit, that the event was about to start, but I found him rising next to me and following me back down to the purple guard ropes.

This close, there was no doubt. The light came from one of the pieces, and one only. The queen. Alderidge's queen.

"Iris," we whispered at the same time. I reached out, without realizing it. An inch or two from the figurine, I felt the frisson run along from my fingertips up my arm. The feeling I'd had every time I'd heard her sing.

"She's in there," I said. Max nodded at my side, his grimace as pained as I felt.

"I think you're right. Nothing we can do about it now, though."

He was right. Numbly, we took our seats. I watched that glow. Iris's glow. It drew me like a beacon. It spoke to me. And I spoke back to it.

*

Neither Rhodes nor Alderidge Claremont came out to play the showcase match, as they usually did. Nor did they even come out to bow and accept praise for their exquisite work. Instead, Merelle took the floor, looking subdued but elegant in a sweeping, gauzy black gown.

"The game of chess is about sacrifice," she said, her eyes scanning the crowd. It felt as though she held my gaze for a long moment that could only have been my imagination. "Just as each piece knows its place is to be sacrificed for the good of the game, sometimes the creator knows they must sacrifice for the sake of their art. Much sacrifice went into the set you see before you. The professors present this set as the pinnacle of their artistic careers, and they have chosen to sacrifice their presence here, so that you may see this board not as a competition between siblings, not as a vehicle for recognition, but as a single work of art that merges three styles, three lives, into one. We invite our recent alumni champions to take the professors' seats and do us the honor of a match."

Two kids slightly older than us, wearing ill-fitting suits, stood up from the front row, shook hands with each other and with Professor Knoll, and sat. They looked nervous, as if this had been sprung on them last minute.

"Oh, of course Claremont's not showing their face." I grabbed Max's hand and got to my feet. "Come on. We're finding that bastard."

The hallway was lined with oil lamps gleaming in glass enclosures, and we each grabbed one without slowing our steps on our way to the metalworking studio.

The door was unlocked, so I pulled it open and stepped inside. The room was empty. Completely empty. Anvil pushed against the wall. Forge dark. Tools packed away somewhere, their pegboards showing only the sooty silhouettes where they used to hang.

We stood, lost. Again, I felt helpless. I knew Alderidge had killed her. I *knew* it. But what could I do about it?

Alderidge had killed Iris and then run. Had Rhodes killed people for his pieces, too? Had they fled together? Where would they have gone? To a new school to start their chess rivalry all over again? But why leave Merelle behind? Unless she was just here to wrap up the tournament, before following them to safety with their precious set and board.

"Sacrifice." The soft voice behind me startled my heart right into my throat, and I whirled around, lantern swaying. Merelle Knoll stood in the doorway, hands clasped contritely, sympathy darkening those come-have-a-hug eyes. "I'm so sorry for your loss, Cosima. Max. I know it's been hard for you. But we all sacrifice for our art. It's best if we do it in silence, behind the scenes, and only let the audience see the beauty. Knowing what goes into it, behind the curtain ... it can burst the magic. The wonder. Alderidge and Rhodes knew that. They sacrificed for this set. It was the best they ever made, and you can be proud in the knowledge that your friend was a part of that."

My eyes misted with tears and rage. I opened my mouth to speak, closed it again. No words would come.

"So, it's true," Max said finally. "They killed her. Are there people in all those other pieces, too?"

Merelle sighed. I didn't know what that sigh meant, but it wasn't surprise, or denial. "I know," the professor continued in that soothing voice. "I know. It's hard. We'll donate this set to the department, okay? You can visit her anytime you want. The most important thing is not to break the bubble for others. We've made her into art. Let them enjoy the beauty of it. All right?"

I met Max's hardened eyes and tightened my hand on the handle of my oil lamp. From my peripheral vision, I saw him do the same.

"She was already art," I said.

As one, we swung our lanterns, bathing Professor Knoll and her gauzy, diaphanous dress in oil and hungry flame.

I fitted the elastic from my corsage against the frame of the big metal door, and Max and I pushed it closed, leaving Merelle Knoll ablaze in the empty metal room. We needed to flee, I knew that, but I couldn't make my feet move. I stood in the flickering dark hall and watched her through the triple-paned glass, flailing and shrieking, not a water bucket left in the abandoned workroom to quench her fires.

Soon, she was a flaming puddle of black gauze on the floor. Soon after that, the flames sputtered out, leaving only smoke and stillness.

And then, almost as one, the lights across campus came on.

Gabrielle Harbowy is an award-nominated editor, an author of three published novels (including *Gears of Faith*, a Pathfinder tie-in novel) and a handful of short stories. She has also written game adventures for D&D and Pathfinder. She is currently a literary agent with Corvisiero Literary Agency. For more information, including her Manuscript Wish List, visit her online at gabrielleharbowy.com.

Pots of a Color Yet Unknown

Cat Rambo

Yes, this is the cloister you have been looking for, the Sisters of Our Lady of the Ultimate, she who holds everything. You have seen so much of it, but there is still more. Let me take you into this building now, where some of us work.

Those red pots are where we keep the fermented leaves, before they're stretched out on the drying screen in the sun, to dry into first soft shreds, then flakes of vegetable matter, pungent with decay and the mold that gourmands claim give it that distinctive flavor and aroma, the ones that make people fly three systems over to come here.

Those orange pots are where we pack the upright stems, soaking them first in brine and then in oil and then rinsing them to begin again, twenty times overall! Most places do it once or twice at most. Ours melt in your mouth and leave behind a trace of salt and vinegar, like standing beside the sea and opening your lips to breathe it in and taste it on your tongue.

Those yellow pots are where we keep the blossoms. When three years of crops have passed through, we will have enough to make a single batch of wine, colored like sunshine and tasting like lying on your back in a meadow and thinking about nothing at all but bee buzz and the wind's soft, meaningless gossip.

Those green pots hold roots; we'll plant them in the spring.

Those blue pots hold seeds, which must never be planted. Strange and flavorless things grow from those seeds and they're hard to eradicate, hard to remove from a field where they've taken grip. Those pots are sealed with wax; in ten years' time, they will be burned, when the smoke is too weak to take root, and even then it will be done on a windy day.

Those indigo pots hold husks of insects, the ones we find lying in the shadows of the leaves, the brittle bits of wing and carapace and pincher. Some addicts powder those, mix them with lemonwater, and drink themselves into unconsciousness, dream themselves into the skies above this planet, dream themselves out of gravity and reality and time, and wake to find they've destroyed their sense of hunger, perhaps a blessing. Perhaps not.

Those purple pots hold the dreams the plants produce, the things they spin in the minds of others, till they come spilling out of their ears and nostrils and mouths. No one wants to give themselves over to that fate, but sometimes they do in spite of that, because of guilt or duty or a sense of common good.

Those clear pots hold nothing; we are still waiting to find out what will fill them. It will happen any day now, they tell me. Until then, I will continue to dip leaves from a red pot, spread them over the fine screen of the mesh, feeling the sun on my shoulders and the distant whine of a ship landing, full of tourists, come to risk addiction for the sake of being able to say they've been here, they know these plants, and that they've returned changed, something other than themselves, hollowed out, refilled. Like a pot whose color is still unknown.

Cat Rambo's 300+ fiction publications include stories in *Asimov's*, *Clarkesworld Magazine*, and *The Magazine of Fantasy and Science Fiction*. In 2020 they won the Nebula Award for fantasy novelette *Carpe Glitter*. They are a former two-term President of the Science Fiction and Fantasy Writers of America (SFWA). Their most recent works are space opera *Devil's Gun* (Tor Macmillan, 2023) and anthology *The Reinvented Detective* (Arc Manor, 2023), coedited with Jennifer Brozek. For more about Cat, as well as links to fiction and popular online school, The Rambo Academy for Wayward Writers, visit www.kittywumpus.net.

Acknowledgments

For nearly three decades, the **Writers' Symposium** has grown from a modest gathering of writers into one of the largest writing events in North America. This would not be possible without the support of Gen Con and the entire gaming community. The Writers' Symposium would like to thank Marian McBrine for her support and encouragement in growing our program these past several years to include projects such as this anthology. And, of course, our thanks to the writers, readers, gamers, and everyone who has participated in our programming, whether as a guest, volunteer, or attendee. We wouldn't exist without you.

Atthis Arts has roots deeply seeded in both the Writers' Symposium and the broader Gen Con community, and publishing this book is a long-realized dream for our small press. We'd like to thank the Writers' Symposium for the opportunity to bring these stories to print and look forward to seeing what the future holds. Atthis Arts especially would like to thank Cat Rambo, Steve Drew, and Gregory A. Wilson for seeing our potential before we were known. And most of all, our thanks to you, for reading these stories. To learn more about us, our values, our community, and our work, please visit atthisarts.com.

Content Notes

The content of this anthology is intended for adults and teens. Specific notes for each story follow. These may reveal elements of the plot, and are intended for readers looking to avoid specific elements prior to reading the stories.

Pages 1-11, "All Time Is Now"
    Occultism, death, seizures

Pages 12-25, "All Things Fixed"
    Blood, death, gore, religion, starvation, violence

Pages 26-39, "Who We Were in the Mirror"
    Language, policing femininity and maternal gatekeeping, family estrangement/tension, grief, fantasy violence, dark humor

Pages 41-54, "Painted World of Witch and Wizard"
    Blood, death, spiders, transmisia

Pages 55-68, "Memento Miri"
    Blood, bones, corpse reanimation, mild profanity

Pages 69-83, "You Need Not Fear"
    Blood, death, gore, fire, violence

Pages 84-92, "Turnkey"
    Demons, fratricide, profanity, religion

Pages 93-114, "One Kind of Many, Undefined by Them"
    Blood, death, kidnapping, profanity, implied sexual assault, slut shaming, violence

Pages 116-127, "Eye of the Beholder"
    Blood, misgendering, off-page murder, profanity, transmisia

Pages 129-139, "The Grandmother Tale"
    Blood, death, fire, gore, mild sensuality, off-page sexual assault, torture, violence, war

Pages 140-154, "For a Thousand Silver Blessings"
    Blood, death, mild profanity, violence, race-based attributes

Pages 155-164, "Kicking Santa's Ass"
    Profanity, mild violence

Pages 165-179, "The Goblin's Locket"
    Faked death, societal racism

Pages 181-192, "Hands Are for Helping"
    Anxiety, mild profanity, seizures, children in peril

Pages 193-207, "All the Light in the Room"
    Off-page ableism (attitude of one of the characters), blood, death, fire, gore, murder

Pages 208-210, "Pots of a Color Yet Unknown"
    Brief mention of religion

Milton Keynes UK
Ingram Content Group UK Ltd.
UKHW020225130824
1238UKWH00001B/39